ONE TRUE WAY

ONE TRUE WAY
one true way
1 ONE TRUE WAY
ONE TRUE WAY
one true way
ONE TRUE WAY
one true way
ONE TRUE WAY
one true way
ONE TRUE WAY

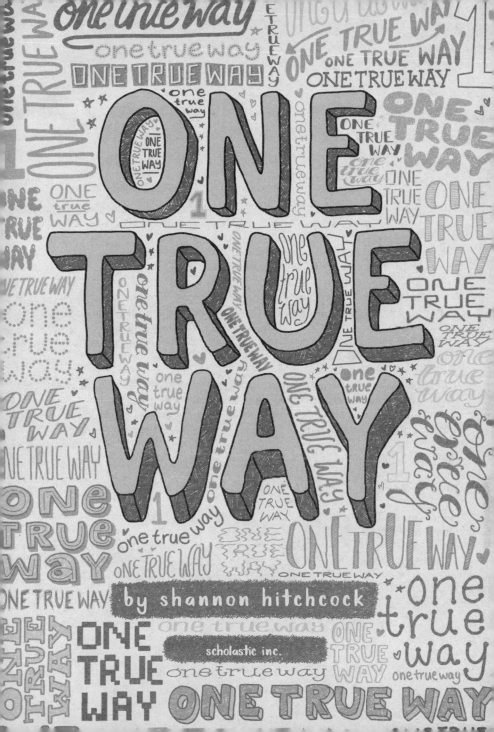

ONE TRUE WAY

by shannon hitchcock

scholastic inc.

ISBN 978-1-338-27970-2

10 9 8 7 6 5 4 3 2 1   18 19 20 21 22

Printed in the U.S.A.   40
First printing 2018

Book design by Maeve Norton

For all the Sams and Allies everywhere.

ONE TRUE WAY

Allie Drake–
Staff Reporter

August—1977

My life was about to change. I had two goals on my first day at Daniel Boone Middle School: make a friend, and join the newspaper staff. It was the perfect job for me. I was a people watcher, a tad nosy, and an excellent typist.

I studied each of the kids in health class, trying to find one who looked friendly. Instead, Samantha Johnson found me. She swung around in her seat and stuck out her hand like a politician. "Just call me Sam," she said. "I know all the kids at DB, so you must be new."

My reporter's antenna went up. This girl had confidence. She was just the kind of kid who would introduce me to her friends. "Allison Drake." My voice came out all scratchy, like I had a frog in my throat.

"Ribbit, ribbit," Sam said.

"Ribbit, ribbit," I answered. I was usually shy around people I didn't know, but something about Sam felt different, right from the start.

"Bet you don't have anybody to sit with at lunch," she said.

If not for her big, toothy smile, I would have been embarrassed to admit it.

"You can eat with me," Sam decided. "Would you rather sit with the jocks, the brains, the theater kids, or the debs? I'm one of the few kids who can sit at any table."

Sam didn't say it in a braggy, I'm-full-of-myself way, but like she was stating facts. "Debs?" I asked.

"Yeah, future debutantes. They're the most popular girls in seventh grade. In a couple of years, they'll be high school cheerleaders, majorettes, and riding convertibles in the Homecoming Parade."

I couldn't imagine anybody who'd have less in common with a deb than Sam. She had on a T-shirt that said *Daniel Boone Pioneers* tucked into her bell-bottoms. Her hair was cut into a wedge, like the figure skater Dorothy Hamill, and she was probably the friendliest person I'd ever met.

Sam was also in my English class, which met right before lunch. She didn't have a pencil or a notebook and slouched down in the seat in front of me.

"What's happening, Sam I Am?" asked a boy with an Afro. He wore a silky shirt with the sleeves rolled up to his elbows, and a comb handle protruded from his back pocket.

"Not much, Dwayne. I won a couple trophies riding Penelope over the summer. Have you met Allison?"

Dwayne shook his head. He had a nice, easy smile.

"Here, Sam," said one of the debs and handed her a pencil and a few sheets of notebook paper.

"Thanks, Kelly. This is Allison."

If you asked me, Kelly looked like all the other debs: long silky hair parted down the middle, perfect teeth, and a cute figure. I was a little envious of her, to be honest.

"Welcome to DB," said a girl with thick red hair. It

flowed in feathered layers that reminded me of my brother's Farrah Fawcett poster. She snapped the rings open on her binder and handed Sam some mimeographed sheets. "Thought you might like a copy of my notes from science class."

Sam flashed her a smile. "Phoebe, if it wouldn't be too much trouble, maybe you could copy your notes every day."

Phoebe nodded so hard her bangs bounced.

I learned three things in English class that day:

1. We were going to read *Johnny Tremain*.

2. Sam was skating through middle school without doing much work. And . . .

3. She had a horse named Penelope.

After class, I followed Sam to the lunchroom. "Did you decide which kids you'd like to sit with?" she asked.

No contest. I wanted to sit with the newspaper kids. "You didn't mention the *Pioneer* staff, but I'd really like to meet them." I planned to be the best reporter in the history of DB Middle School.

"Okay," Sam said. "We'll sit across from Webster. He's the editor in chief."

I barely had time to say how Webster was a great name for an editor before Sam had slapped down her brown paper bag. "Hey, Webb. This is my friend Allison. She's new at DB."

Webster and I had a lot in common, I could already tell. Both of us had thick blond bangs that we liked to hide behind, wire-rimmed glasses, and, judging from the newspaper spread out in front of him, a love for reading.

"Nice to meet you," Webster said. "Sam, did your mom bake chocolate chip cookies? I'll trade you a bag of chips for a cookie."

Sam reached into her sack and handed him a cookie. "Keep your chips, Webb. I need a favor."

Webb bit into the cookie. "Ummm," he said and a look of pure chocolate bliss spread across his face. "What's the favor?"

I leaned toward him. "The favor is for me. I used to work on our school newspaper in New Jersey, and I want to be a reporter here too."

"Normally, I request a writing sample."

I would have shown him a hundred samples, but Sam handed Webb another cookie. "I know you have strict rules, but let's cut through the red tape on account of Allie's new. She can interview me about winning a trophy at the Pinto World Championship Horse Show. My mom took great pictures."

"Done!" Webb said. "If Allie turns in a good interview with pictures, she can join my team."

I was usually called Allison because Mom hated nicknames, but I didn't correct them. I liked the sound of it—Allie Drake, Staff Reporter.

How Do You Explain a Dead Brother?

I waited on the bleachers for Sam to finish basketball practice. I scribbled interview questions, noting that she played point guard. I sketched the way her hair bounced as she dribbled. She was beautiful. No, that wasn't exactly the right word. She was . . . handsome. Usually, I wouldn't describe a girl as handsome, but in Sam's case it fit.

At the sound of Coach Murphy's whistle, Sam drove toward the basket. Gliding through the air, she scored a layup. How'd she do that? I didn't have an athletic bone in my body.

When practice was over, Sam headed for the locker room. About twenty minutes later, she climbed the bleachers with a towel slung around her neck. "Want to go to my house? You can interview me after supper."

I wanted to go home with Sam like a normal kid, but my mom would have had a stroke. She'd been overprotective since my brother died. "Uh . . . I can't, but maybe you could go home with me?"

"Sure," Sam said. "Lead the way."

The house we'd rented was only a couple of blocks from school. I carried an armload of books, while Sam dribbled her basketball down the street. Her hair was damp from the shower she had taken after practice, and mine was damp from the North Carolina heat.

"Thanks for introducing me to Webb. Being a reporter means a lot to me."

"No problem," Sam said. She dribbled the basketball between her legs. "Do you have any brothers and sisters?"

I never knew how to answer that question. Should

I just say no because Eric was gone? Or should I say yes and leave it at that? Or simply tell the truth? There is no easy way to explain a dead brother.

"Well, do you?" Sam asked.

"Nope. It's only me." That answer caused a guilty conscience, but telling the truth would have made me cry. I was sick of crying. I wanted to be a regular kid again. "What about you?"

Sam's whole face lit up. "I have an older sister and a younger brother. Melissa's a sophomore at DBH and Jonathan's only five. He's cute and funny. You'll love him!"

For just a minute, I was so jealous I wished I hadn't met Sam. Kids who have brothers and sisters don't know how lucky they are, but to be fair, I didn't know either, not until Eric died.

"My dad farms," Sam continued, "and my mom's a church secretary. What about yours?"

"Uh . . . my mom's the new librarian here in town, and Dad's still living in New Jersey." What I didn't say was they'd probably get a divorce, and I blamed Dad. We used to be a perfect family: Dad, Mom, Eric, and me. I even had the pictures to prove it.

While I unlocked the door, Sam kept bouncing her ball. I wondered why she couldn't relax. Where did all that nervous energy come from?

Our den was full of boxes from our move. I started to apologize for the mess, but the words clumped together like saltwater taffy. While I had been at school, Mom had hung our family portrait over the fireplace. She believed Dad would come back to us, but I didn't need another reminder that both he and Eric were gone. Every day their empty seats at the kitchen table stole my appetite. My bottom lip trembled. I tried to make it stop, but I couldn't control it. "I use—used to have a family."

Sam turned me around so I didn't have to see the portrait. "You look like a lost puppy."

The tone of her voice was gentle. Sam understood. For the first time since Eric had died, somebody was solely focused on me. Mom and Dad had been so caught up in their own grief that I had become invisible. My glasses fogged from my tears.

Sam took them off my face and wiped the lenses on her T-shirt. "I don't know exactly what happened, but I do want to be your friend."

She'd seen me cry, but liked me anyway. It seemed

like a minor miracle. I left her and ran to the bath-room to wash my face.

"You okay in there?"

When I opened the door, Sam was staring up at my family's portrait with her hands on her hips. "I called my mom. It's okay if I stay for supper."

I was relieved she still wanted to stay. It was proof I hadn't scared her away. "My mom's working late. You want a sandwich?"

Sam wrinkled her nose. "Not really. I'm always starved after basketball practice. How about I cook?"

That was fine by me, though I'd never had a friend offer to make dinner before. I led the way to the kitchen and watched Sam whip up omelets. My only contributions were setting the table and pouring orange juice.

Sam focused on her omelet and didn't ask me any questions. Finally, I couldn't stand the silence. "Eric died in a car accident. I hate telling people because then they feel sorry for me, and it gets all weird."

Sam stood and put more bread into the toaster. "I'm sorry it happened, and I promise not to get all weird." She shrugged. "At least not any weirder than I already am."

"Can I ask you a question?"

Sam grabbed the toast that had just popped up. "Sure."

"Why is Phoebe copying her notes for you?"

"Oh, that." Sam reached for a knife and spread butter on her toast. "It's embarrassing."

"Tell me anyway."

"I'm a bad student, but a pretty good athlete. My friends help out so I can play on the basketball team."

"Are you doing your absolute best?"

"Uh . . . I hadn't really thought about it."

"I have. I think you're smart, but taking the easy way out."

Sam grinned. "Maybe."

"I'll help you too, but only if you promise to try really hard."

Sam nodded. "I like you, Allie Drake. None of my other friends would've said that."

"I like you too. A lot."

I took charge of washing dishes while Sam dried. She loved to cook, but didn't much like cleaning up.

About fifteen minutes later, Mom came home. "Mom, this is my new friend, Samantha Johnson."

"Just call me Sam," she said.

I took a seat at the kitchen table and watched Sam use her charm. Not only did she make Mom an omelet, Sam borrowed my glasses, shook her hair into her face, and imitated Webster. "Chocolate chip cookies," she said. "I don't need a writing sample from Allie. For two cookies, she can be editor in chief."

Mom laughed. "Sam, I think you could sell ice to an Eskimo."

"I don't know any Eskimos," Sam said, "but could I talk you into letting Allie go to my house tomorrow?"

Mom held her hand up like she was fending off an attacker. "We still have unpacking to do, and I . . . I haven't met your parents."

"Please, Mom. Sam will give you the number, and you can talk to her mom ahead of time."

"But . . ."

"I need to make new friends. Don't you want me to be happy here?"

She sighed. "No promises, but I'll call Mrs. Johnson."

I was one step closer to being a regular kid again.

Coach Murphy

The next day reminded me of a Carly Simon song. It was all about the *"Anticipation"* of going to Sam's house. I wanted a new best friend almost as much as I wanted to be a reporter.

In health class, Coach Murphy announced we'd be studying the musculoskeletal system. She taught us in an unusual way—by playing an imaginary basketball game with Sam.

Coach dribbled a pretend ball.

Sam lunged and tried to steal it.

Coach threw an elbow.

"I'm calling foul on that one," Dwayne said.

"Exactly," Coach said, "but because of her ribs, Sam didn't get hurt. What organs do our ribs protect?"

"Lungs!" Phoebe said.

"What else?"

"Heart," said one of the debs.

Coach raised her elbow to the side of Sam's head. "Sam's brain is protected by her . . ."

"Skull," somebody shouted.

The whole class period was like that. Coach made learning fun. Maybe she'd give me a couple of quotes about Sam. Quotes always jazz up an article. I'd ask her after school.

In English class, I fidgeted as much as Sam. Not even historical fiction could take my mind off going home with her.

At lunch, Sam wanted to sit with the jocks. She took a seat in front of Dwayne Williams. "Big D, you think the Tar Heels are gonna be any good this year?"

"The Tar Heels are a sure thing," Dwayne said. "Coach Smith will have those boys whipped into shape."

I didn't have much to say because I didn't know the first thing about college basketball. My mom had warned me it was like a religion in North Carolina, and I should have paid attention. I didn't know any of the players that Sam and Dwayne discussed, but I decided to become best friends with the sports page.

When the long school day finally ended, I headed for Coach Murphy's office. I gave a quick knock and pushed the door open. Miss Holt, our English teacher, was standing very close to Coach, and she was crying.

Coach's eyes darted from Miss Holt to me. "Can I help you, Allison?"

Both teachers looked uncomfortable, like I'd walked into a dressing room where they were changing clothes. "Uh, well, I'm writing a profile about Sam Johnson for the school paper. I thought maybe you could give me a couple of quotes."

Coach nodded. "Let me think about it. I'll jot something down, and we can talk tomorrow."

I backed out the door. I didn't know what was wrong with Miss Holt, or why I'd made them feel so uncomfortable, but my reporter's antenna was humming. I planned to find out.

Sam lived about five miles outside of town, and we took the late bus to her house. Those five miles made a big difference. Instead of a house on a tree-lined street, Sam lived on twenty-five acres. When I saw her family's barn and pasture, I quoted a line from *Big Red Barn*: "By the big red barn/In the great green field . . ."

Sam nodded. "My brother loves that book." She pointed toward the barn. "Do you want to meet people or horses first?"

"Definitely people." No way Mom would have let me visit if she'd known about the horses. I'd tried not to let her fears affect me, but they had. I'd always been cautious, but lately it was more than that. I expected something else bad to happen at any moment.

When Sam pushed open the back door, a small body barreled into her. "Hey, Jon Jon," she said and lifted him into the air.

"Can we play horse?" he asked.

Sam winked at me and dropped to her knees. Jonathan scrambled onto her back and grabbed hold of Sam's shirt. Neighing like a horse, Sam crawled from the mudroom into the kitchen. I tagged along behind.

Sam's older sister looked up from the books she had spread across the kitchen table. "Hi, I'm Melissa."

Melissa and Sam had the same dark hair and eyes, but they didn't look at all alike. Melissa was thin and willowy. She had on makeup, and her fingernails were painted. Melissa was a deb. "Nice to meet you. I'm Allie Drake." It amazed me that the same parents had daughters as different from each other as Sam and Melissa.

When Jonathan finally got tired of playing horse, Sam and I climbed the stairs to her bedroom. An entire wall was covered in bookshelves, but instead of books, the shelves held ribbons, trophies, and pictures of Sam. In some of them she was riding her horse; in others she was playing basketball.

Sam plopped down on the plaid quilt covering one of the twin beds. "The Pinto World Championship Horse Show is in Tulsa, Oklahoma," she said.

"You went all the way to Oklahoma to ride in a horse show?"

Sam grinned. "Yeah, my mom thought it was a crazy idea, but my dad loves horses as much as I do. The whole family went except for Melissa."

I picked up a picture from the shelf of Sam wearing chaps and an enormous belt buckle. "Guess you have to dress the part."

"Yep, and your horse has to look good too. When Penelope was first born, I noticed her coat was as shiny as a new penny. That's where her name comes from."

"She's a beautiful horse."

"I'll teach you to ride her," Sam said.

I shook my head. "My mom would worry that I'd get hurt."

Sam sat up and leaned against the headboard. "You could fall down the stairs on the way to supper, or slip in the bathtub, or get bit by a rabid raccoon. If you're afraid all the time, you'll never have any fun."

Sam looked so serious. "A rabid raccoon, huh? Are there a lot of those around?"

"I've never met one yet," Sam said. "That's my whole point. You're wasting time worrying over things that will never happen."

That was the difference between us. Nothing bad had ever touched Sam's family, but since Eric had died, my safety net had a huge hole in it. "I stopped by Coach Murphy's office to get a quote for our interview, but something strange happened."

Sam leaned forward and rested her elbows on her knees. "What?"

"Coach was with Miss Holt, and I got a weird feeling. Like I'd interrupted something private."

Sam looked away. "Coach is my best friend. At least, she's my best adult friend. When I first met her, I knew we were alike."

"Because you both like sports?"

"Yeah, something like that. Don't mention what you saw to anyone else, okay?"

The way Sam's voice sounded, serious and sad, made me even more curious. "I promise, but can you tell me why?"

Sam shook her head. "I asked Coach a hard question, and she told me the truth. I can't break her trust in me." She climbed off the bed. "Do you smell hamburgers? I bet Mom could use some help in the kitchen."

I was left holding a picture of Penelope while Sam clambered down the steps. She knew something about Coach and Miss Holt that I didn't. That was my first clue.

Not Special Enough

I stood in the kitchen doorway while Sam slapped slices of American cheese on the burgers. "Mom, this is my friend Allie Drake."

Mrs. Johnson had teased hair, the kind that requires a weekly beauty shop appointment. She opened a jar of mayonnaise and spooned a large glob into a bowl of diced potatoes. "Glad you could stay to supper."

Sam complained that we were having potato salad, but I didn't mind at all. With the red-checked tablecloth, it seemed like a picnic.

Outside the kitchen window, a deep voice sang "Hello, Darlin'."

"Who's the Conway Twitty imitator?" I asked. I'd been listening to the local radio station and singing with a twang to make Mom laugh. The music and the accent were so different from what we'd listened to in New Jersey.

"It's my dad," Sam groaned. "He thinks he's a country music star."

Mr. Johnson waltzed into the kitchen with Jonathan following him. He kissed Sam on the cheek and hugged Mrs. Johnson from behind. It was easy to see who Sam got her personality from. "You must be Allie," he said. "Jonathan told me you were staying for supper."

"I hope that's okay."

His eyes twinkled. "Of course it is. There's never a shortage of food around here."

I sat across from Sam and didn't say much during dinner. No, make that supper. Southerners called it supper. Mostly, I watched Sam's family and thought how different it was from a quiet meal with Mom. Sam and her father actually arm wrestled for the last burger.

. "I declare a tie," Mr. Johnson said. "Looks like we'll have to split the burger."

"You two beat all I've ever seen," Mrs. Johnson said. "Allie will think we're a bunch of heathens."

"What's a heathen?" Jonathan asked.

"Somebody who's uncivilized," Melissa answered. "Like you when you chew with your mouth open or forget to use your napkin."

Jonathan grabbed his napkin and put it in his lap.

Everybody laughed, but not in a making-fun-of-him way. They all adored him. I could tell.

Mrs. Johnson said, "That's enough talk about heathens. Allie, have you and your mom found a church? We'd surely love to have you at One True Way."

Sam pushed some potato salad around with her fork. She had the same tense expression as when I asked her about Coach and Miss Holt. My reporter's antenna hummed. Could there be a connection between One True Way and our teachers? "We're Methodists," I said, "but maybe I could visit your church sometime."

When Mom came to pick me up, Mrs. Johnson was reading her Bible. She marked her place and followed Sam and me to the front porch. While our moms chatted, I said to Sam, "I'm gonna start reading the sports page."

"Why?"

"So we'll have something in common."

Sam laughed. "I like that we're different."

"You do?"

"Yeah, it's nice. Just be who you are, Allie. I think you're pretty special."

My cheeks felt warm, even in the night air.

On the drive home, Mom stared straight ahead with both hands gripping the steering wheel, her knuckles white. "It's so dark out. Hard to see."

She had a point. There were no streetlights on these winding country roads. Mom had never been a confident driver, but it was much worse since Eric's death. I knew the only reason she had agreed to drive at night was so I could make friends. While I'd been having fun, she had had dinner alone. That's the kind of thing I would've never worried about when there were four of us, but now Mom was all I had and vice versa.

I knew Eric didn't mean to wreck our car, but he shouldn't have been driving so fast. If he hadn't, I'd still have a brother, Dad would still be living with us, and we would have never moved from New Jersey.

It seemed Mom could read my mind. "Dad called you tonight."

I hated him. I didn't answer and stared out the window into the darkness. It wasn't my fault or Mom's that Eric died, but Dad had left us anyway. I scrunched my eyes closed and admitted the truth. I didn't really hate Dad. I remembered what Sam had said. *Just be who you are, Allie. I think you're pretty special.* But if I was so special, why had Dad left me? And more important, how could I get him back?

Allie Drake-
Private Tutor

I was daydreaming about Sam when Coach Murphy asked me to stay after class.

She stood in front of her desk and fiddled with the whistle around her neck. "Look, Allie, I'm sorry about yesterday. Miss Holt's mom fell and broke her hip. She was telling me about it when you walked in."

"Oh, I knew it was something private. Sorry." That solved half the mystery, but it didn't explain why Sam had asked me not to talk about it. My reporter's antenna went up. There was more to this story.

Coach reached into the jacket of her nylon tracksuit and handed me a folded piece of paper. "This is the quote you wanted. Go ahead and read it. Make sure it's all right."

I unfolded it and read: *Sam Johnson is the most talented point guard I've coached in twenty years. Her big heart and outgoing personality make her a leader both on and off the basketball court.*

"It's great!"

Coach smiled. "My pleasure. Sam is really something special."

I couldn't have agreed more.

After school, I hurried home to the Smith Corona typewriter Mom had given me last Christmas. I put in a clean sheet of paper and started my article: *"Sam Johnson—A Star On and Off the Court."* In my opening paragraph, I wrote about meeting Sam on my first day at DB. I admitted how nervous I'd been about eating lunch alone, but that Sam had introduced me to Webster. I told about watching her practice basketball, how she glided through the air scoring a layup. I dropped in the quote from Coach and added a couple paragraphs about the Pinto World Championship Horse Show. I even threw in how she had arm wrestled her dad at the dinner table. I ended the article this way: *Whether on or off the court, Sam Johnson makes every day more interesting at Daniel Boone Middle School.*

While I was proofreading and erasing my mistakes, the phone rang. I ran to the hall to answer it.

"Hey, it's me," Sam said. "What are you doing?"

"Working on a story about my favorite star athlete."

"Good. I'm way more interesting than Johnny Tremain. He is one boring dude."

"Promise you won't laugh at me."

"Cross my heart."

"Yeah, but do you cross your heart and hope to die, stick a pin in your eye?"

"I do," Sam said. "What's the big confession?"

"I love *Johnny Tremain*. The way it takes you to another time and place."

"I officially declare you the smartest person I know," Sam said. "Except for Webb. He's a brain too. Are you sure you want to be my friend?"

"I'm sure."

Sam and I sat breathing into our phones. We didn't have much in common, but it didn't seem to matter. "Maybe I could tutor you in English."

"I'll make a deal with you," Sam said. "You can tutor me in English, and I'll teach you to ride Penelope."

My heart slammed against my chest. I was afraid of Penelope, but I wanted to impress Sam. I'd have to trust her not to laugh at me or let me get hurt, and I'd have to hide it from Mom. "It has to be a secret. My mom wouldn't like it. Not one bit."

"I won't tell her," Sam said, "but won't she notice when your clothes get dusty and you smell like a horse?"

If I wanted to be a normal kid again, I had to take some risks. "No problem. I'll bring old clothes to change into and some perfume." In my best Monty Hall imitation, I shouted, "Let's make a deal!"

The next morning, I hurried to Miss Holt's classroom for an early meeting with Webb. He'd brought Krispy Kreme doughnuts, which put me in an outstanding mood.

While I licked jelly off my fingers, Webb read through my article. When he got to the end, he put the second page down and started reading the first page again. "Webster, you're driving me crazy. Do you like it or not?"

Webb pushed his glasses up. "It needs a little more depth. Highlight the coach/player relationship. You tell us how Coach Murphy feels about Sam, but how does Sam feel about her coach?"

He was right. I thought I'd turned in a perfect article. I'd even had Mom proofread so it wouldn't have any mistakes. "I can fix it, Webb. Do you think I'm good enough to join your staff?"

"You don't mind revising?"

"I wish it had been good enough the first time, but I know revision is part of the process."

"Revision is the magic word!" Webster said. "Allie Drake, you're hired. The pay is zero, the hours are long, but on the plus side you'll get to work with a handsome devil like me."

That Webster had a real sense of humor. "Doughnuts, Webb. I'll work for jelly doughnuts."

Allie Drake-
Deep Thinker

I ran home after school bursting with good news. "Mom," I shouted as soon as I pushed the door open.

She hurried from the kitchen wiping her hands on a dish towel. "Somebody sounds happy."

I proceeded to tell her the whole story. How Webb liked my article, but I had to revise. Mom's face glowed. It was the same look she used to get when Eric hit a home run or picked flowers for her. She hadn't looked happy in a long time.

"That's wonderful news," she said. "I'm proud of you, Allison."

"Would you call me Allie?"

Mom's eyebrows shot up. "What brought this on? Allison is a beautiful name."

"Allie is my byline. Allie Drake—Staff Reporter." I waited for an argument, but didn't get one.

"I'll try and remember to call you Allie. Reverend Walker says, well, she says I have to loosen up. The way I've treated you since Eric died is not exactly healthy."

That was putting it mildly. Mom was smothering me. "So you went to counseling today?"

Mom nodded. "I need to talk about Eric." She clutched the dish towel over her heart. "It's all bottled up in here, and if I don't get it out, I'll suffocate."

What she didn't say was talking had pushed Dad away. After Eric died, the more she talked about him, the later Dad stayed at work. He wanted to pretend like nothing had happened. One night I'd heard him yell, "What good does talking do? We can't fix it!"

"Allison . . . I mean, Allie, maybe you'd like to talk to Reverend Walker. Eric's death and what happened with your dad has been hard on you too."

I liked having a woman minister. I liked it a lot, but I wasn't sure about counseling, at least not yet.

"Let me think about it." The smell of lemon and fresh herbs wafted through the house. "Roast chicken?"

"You have your dad's nose for food. Since it's Friday, I've invited Reverend Walker, Coach Murphy, and Franny Holt for dinner."

"How do you know my teachers?"

"Silly question," Mom said. "Teachers use the library all the time. Do you mind that I included them?"

Mind? I was thrilled! That would give me a chance to observe Coach and Miss Holt together again. Maybe I could even solve the other half of the mystery. "Don't worry, Mom. I'm looking forward to it."

Hosting a dinner party was a big deal for Mom. She used to love entertaining, but hadn't made the effort since Eric died. When I saw fresh flowers and candles on the dining room table, I showered and changed into a dress. I wanted my mom back. She hadn't actually gone away, not like Dad, but she hadn't been herself either. A dinner party seemed like a positive sign.

Reverend Walker was the first to arrive. She had

the smile of an angel. Seriously, it lit up her whole face. She thrust a long Pyrex dish into my hands. "I brought a Coca-Cola cake for dessert."

I'd never heard of such a cake. It was bound to be another strange Southern food like grits or black-eyed peas. My palate was definitely expanding.

I carried the cake into the dining room and placed it on the sideboard. I heard Reverend Walker say to Mom, "I'm happy you followed my suggestion. Finding something to look forward to every day is one of the keys to feeling better."

I slipped into my room and pulled out my journal. I jotted down, *Find Something to Look Forward to Every Day*. Underneath it I wrote one name: *Sam*. She was better than hearing a favorite song on the radio or slurping a cherry coke.

When the doorbell rang for a second time, I hurried to answer it. Coach Murphy and Miss Holt stood outside. Both women fit their job descriptions. Coach was tall and muscled, while Miss Holt was small and bookish.

Coach handed me a Tupperware container cold enough to freeze my fingers off. "Homemade ice cream. Cranked the freezer myself."

"It's wonderful with Coca-Cola cake," Miss Holt added. "I'd pop it in the freezer until after dinner."

Reverend Walker must have planned dessert with them—ice cream to go with her cake. "Thank you," I said. The frog was back in my throat because they were being so nice to us.

All three women crowded into the kitchen with Mom. She tried to shoo them away while she finished dinner, but they weren't having it. Reverend Walker stirred the gravy, Coach carved the chicken, and Miss Holt rummaged in the junk drawer for matches. Maybe Mom had it all wrong when she'd shut herself away in the house and the library. Having people around wouldn't bring Eric back, but it might help with her loneliness.

After Miss Holt lit the candles, we held hands around the dinner table. Reverend Walker prayed:

"Gracious Lord,

We thank you for the gifts of food and friendship. Bless my old friends Murph and Franny and my new friends Elizabeth and Allison.

Amen."

I didn't say much while the grown-ups chatted

about how they'd spent their summers. Instead I watched Coach and Miss Holt with a reporter's eye. I wanted to figure out what Sam wouldn't tell me.

"Everybody should see the Grand Canyon at least once," Coach said.

"It's spectacular," Miss Holt agreed. "I would have never ridden a burro in the canyon, but Murph insisted." She laughed. "And the year before that she talked me into scuba diving lessons."

"I'm not sure I could be talked into either of those things," Mom said, "but it sounds like you enjoyed them."

"You should see the pictures Franny took of the Grand Canyon," Reverend Walker said. "She's a gifted photographer."

"I'd like to see those pictures." I hadn't meant to blurt that out, but I liked taking pictures too.

"Everybody's invited to our house for a cookout," Coach said. "You can see the pictures then."

I had an aha moment. Coach had said *our house.* She and Miss Holt were roommates. The only other adults I knew who lived together without being married were Dad's brother, Jeffrey, and his boy-friend, Dominic.

After dinner, Mom brewed coffee for the adults and heated apple cider with a cinnamon stick for me. I kept watching Coach and Miss Holt. They looked at each other in a different way from how they looked at Mom or Reverend Walker.

"Dwayne." Coach snapped her fingers twice. "I can't remember that kid's last name."

"Williams," said Miss Holt.

"Yeah, Dwayne Williams. Unless I miss my guess, he and Sam Johnson will both be standouts in high school."

"Sam is a natural salesman," Reverend Walker added. "Every year she sells me magazines I don't have time to read and candy I don't need to eat."

"I like Sam," Mom said. "I'm glad she and Allie are friends."

"Sam is the most interesting person I've ever met," I said.

Mom set her cup down on the coffee table and stared at me. "I didn't realize you liked Sam more than your New Jersey friends."

I felt my face heat up. It was bound to be the color of a ripe tomato.

Once we'd said good night to our guests, Mom asked me to help clean the kitchen. I grabbed a dish towel, while she stood at the sink scrubbing the roasting pan. "Mom, are Coach and Miss Holt . . . you know . . . together?"

Mom dropped the roasting pan in the white porcelain sink. The noise the pan made echoed like my question. "What?"

"Are they together?" I repeated.

Mom turned off the faucet and swiveled to face me. "Where did that question come from?"

"From watching them at dinner. They remind me of a married couple. The way they smile at each other and go on vacations together. You know . . . stuff like that."

Mom leaned against the sink. She gazed up at the ceiling and took a deep breath. "They're like Uncle Jeffrey and Dom."

Dad's brother was gay, but nobody ever talked about it. "You don't mind?"

"No, if I did, I wouldn't have invited them to dinner." Mom tucked a strand of hair behind her ear.

"Not everyone in town is quite so open-minded, though. This is not a topic to discuss with your friends."

"Why?"

Mom sighed. "Because gossip could jeopardize their jobs. Like Anita Bryant and that Save Our Children campaign. Some people will do anything to stop gays from living in their communities."

Anita Bryant was a Christian celebrity, a former beauty queen, who sold orange juice on TV. She thought gay people were a bad influence on kids and shouldn't be teachers. I'd heard Walter Cronkite talk about her on the evening news. "But Anita Bryant's in Florida."

"That's right," Mom said, "but her influence is spreading. Our state senator, Jesse Helms, has pledged his support. It's better to let people turn a blind eye and pretend Murph and Franny are just roommates."

"But that's a lie."

Mom gave me a hug. "It would have been easier for Franny and Murph if they'd fallen in love with men, but that's not what happened."

I rested my head against Mom's shoulder. It

was nice to be treated like an almost-grown-up. "Mom, you fell in love with Dad, but that hasn't been easy either."

Mom sighed again. "You're a deep thinker, Allie Drake."

Horses Don't
Judge

That same weekend, Sam and I waved good-bye as Mom's Dodge Dart disappeared in a cloud of red dust. Sam wanted to go to the barn, but I insisted on homework first.

Sam led the way to her bedroom. As soon as she closed the door, I blurted out, "I know about Coach and Miss Holt."

"Ssssh," Sam whispered. She grabbed an album from the stack on her bookshelf and put *Frampton Comes Alive!* on her record player. She turned up the volume. "Now we can talk."

Sam and I lay on the floor facing each other. I told her about Mom's dinner party. How I had watched Coach and Miss Holt, and about my talk with Mom after they'd gone home.

"I've known for a couple of months," Sam said. "Your mom's right. Most people pretend they're just roommates."

That gave me a sad, achy feeling. The same way I felt when I thought about Dad.

"At least they have the guts to be together," Sam said. "Think about it that way." She jumped to her feet and played air guitar along with Peter Frampton. "C'mon."

I shook my head, afraid I'd look silly.

"How about a duet?" Sam asked.

She kept on until I gave in. We belted out "Show Me the Way" like two seventh-grade rock stars. I was self-conscious, but only a little bit. I wanted to spend every spare minute with Sam. When I was away from home, it was easier to forget about Eric and Dad.

"See, that wasn't so bad."

After making popcorn, Sam and I went back to

her room to study *Johnny Tremain*. "The language is so old-fashioned," she complained.

"Yeah, but that's part of the fun. Listen while I imitate Mrs. Lapham."

When I finished reading, Sam clapped. "You should try out for the school play. I bet you'd get a part."

I threw a piece of popcorn at her. "I'd probably pee my pants or die of stage fright."

Sam laughed and threw a handful of popcorn at me. "I bet you'd be great."

I wished I had as much confidence in myself as Sam had in me. Maybe that's why I liked her so much. Around her, I forgot to be scared.

After we finished our homework, Sam and I ran toward the fenced-in pasture. Sweat trickled down my back. It was a lot hotter in North Carolina than in New Jersey.

Sam leaned against the gate. She put her fingers to her lips and gave a shrill whistle. Penelope galloped toward us. I had to admit she was even more beautiful than in pictures.

"Hey, Penny. How you doing, girl?" The horse pricked her ears toward Sam and lowered her head. Sam climbed onto the lowest rung of the gate so she could reach over and hug her. "Penny's my best friend in the world."

It was silly to be jealous of a horse, but I wanted to be Sam's best friend. "You have a million friends at school. Why do you like Penny more than them?"

"Horses don't judge," Sam said. "Penny doesn't care that I dress like a boy, or about my report card, or if I miss the winning basket. Penny just loves me."

The breeze had blown Sam's hair into her eyes. I wanted to take my fingers and brush it back, but I didn't. "If you're worried about your clothes, I could go shopping with you."

Sam shook her head. "I'm more comfortable this way. I feel stupid in a dress."

She went on petting Penelope and didn't look at me. I needed to say something, but it had to be just right. "I wouldn't change a single thing about you. Not one."

"Really?"

"Yeah, because of you I'm on the newspaper staff,

and I'm brave enough to ride a horse . . . at least I think I am."

Sam reached for my hand. She held it for a couple of seconds before placing it on Penelope's neck. "No riding today. You and Penny need to get to know each other first."

"Okay." My voice came out all scratchy again.

"Ribbit, ribbit," Sam said.

I cleared my throat. "Ribbit, ribbit," I answered.

Sam was my best friend, and I hoped someday I'd be hers too.

Allie Drake–
Cheerleading
Expert

Sunday afternoon was warm enough that Mom and I lounged on the front porch swing. She was reading a book Reverend Walker had recommended about dealing with grief. *Johnny Tremain* lay across my lap, but I was thinking about Sam—how because of her, I had tried new things, like singing out loud and spending time with a horse.

When the phone rang, I raced to answer it. It was only Webster.

"I wanted to remind you about tomorrow's news-paper staff meeting."

"I'll be there."

"How's your revision coming along?"

"All finished. I think you'll like it."

"Excellent. You're a pleasure to work with, Allie Drake."

I danced down the hall like a teenager on *American Bandstand*. The pleasure was all mine. I could hardly wait to write another story. "What's my next assignment?"

"I'm working on it," Webb said. "Don't worry. It'll be a good one."

I hung up the phone and danced out to the porch. "Somebody's in a much better mood," Mom said.

"Webb said I'm a pleasure to work with."

"That's wonderful, Allie. I'm so proud of you!"

I danced back toward the door.

"Where are you going now?" Mom asked.

"To call Sam!" Telling her would make my good news even better.

.   .   .

Before school the next morning, I met Webb in Miss Holt's office. He slid two desks together and spread the papers from his briefcase across them. Dwayne Williams and I sat facing him.

Webb pushed his glasses up with two fingers, but they slid back down. "What have you got for me, Big D?"

Dwayne handed him some neatly typed pages. "A recap of football season and my predictions for basketball."

"Excellent," Webb said. "I'll proof these and get back to you. What byline do you want me to use?"

"Same as last year, Dwayne Williams—Roving Sports Reporter."

When it was my turn, I handed in my revision.

Webb quickly read through it. "This is excellent, Allie." He read it through a second time more slowly. "I didn't catch a single mistake. Not one. Which means you're ready for your next assignment."

"My pencil is sharpened and my notebook is handy. What is it?"

"How about interviewing Kelly Hutton?" Webb said.

Kelly was the deb who was always giving Sam paper to take notes. "Okay, anything I should know about her?"

"She's head cheerleader and full of school spirit. Wait until you see her at a pep rally!"

"She's as nice as she is pretty," Dwayne said.

At first glance, Kelly was just another deb, but that would make writing about her more of a challenge. I'd have to keep my eyes open and search for an angle. I didn't want to stereotype her or have Webb say the article needed more depth. I wanted him to see I could take criticism and improve. "Got it. I'll have a profile by next Monday."

In English class, Sam stared out the window. I wondered what she was thinking about. An old song Dad used to sing drifted through my mind, "Dream a Little Dream of Me." Neither Dad nor me had any musical talent, but we both loved listening to records. It was our thing to do together.

Miss Holt rapped her knuckles on her desk. "Sam, can you explain what an apprentice is and how it relates to *Johnny Tremain*?"

Sam turned away from the window. "Sorry. I was watching some kids play dodgeball."

A few of our classmates giggled, but Miss Holt ignored them and cut Sam a break. "What is an apprentice and how does it relate to our story?"

Sam nodded. "Oh, I know that one. An apprentice is like a student. Johnny was learning to be a silversmith."

Miss Holt pressed her palms to her cheeks. A big smile spread across her face. "That's a good answer. A very good answer."

When Miss Holt called on Dwayne for the next question, Sam shifted in her seat and looked at me. "Thanks," she whispered.

I was happier than if I'd aced the question myself.

I spent the rest of English class watching Kelly Hutton. Her long silky hair was parted down the middle. It was so shiny she could have been a Breck Girl in one of the shampoo ads. But what was she really like? That's what the reporter in me needed to know.

I waited on Sam after class. "Miss Holt was shocked when you knew the right answer."

Sam grinned. "I was expecting her to have a Fred Sanford moment. You know, when he grabs his chest and fakes a heart attack."

Sanford and Son was a really funny television show. I pictured Fred, with his big tummy, wearing suspenders, and laughed.

Sam punched me in the arm. "Thanks again. You're the only reason I can even pronounce 'Johnny Tremain.'"

Sam was smarter than she gave herself credit for, but she did struggle to pay attention. My goofy imitation of Mrs. Lapham had helped with that.

"Hey, Allie. Where do you want to sit at lunch?"

"How about with the cheerleaders?"

"You want to join the squad?" Sam joked.

"I'm not nearly coordinated enough, but I, Allie Drake, pledge to become a cheerleading expert. Webb wants me to interview Kelly Hutton."

Kelly Hutton-
Head Deb

When we sat down at the lunch table across from Kelly, she turned her dazzling smile on Sam. "Hi, Allison. Hey, Sammy. It's been a while since you had lunch with me."

Sam reached into her brown bag and pulled out a ham-and-cheese sandwich. "Been making the rounds."

"Hi, Kelly." The frog was back in my throat again.

"Ribbit, ribbit," Sam said.

"Ribbit, ribbit," I answered. "Sorry, sometimes I sound like a frog."

Kelly laughed. "Sometimes I sound like a chicken. Want to hear me?"

I nodded and the future debutante let out a loud *"Bauk, bauk, bauk, bauk, bauk."*

Sam joined in, but I just watched. That's how a reporter gets the scoop, by paying attention to the details. The noise spread from kid to kid, from lunch table to lunch table. Pretty soon most of the seventh grade was clucking and cock-a-doodle-dooing.

Coach Murphy blew her whistle until they stopped being chickens and went back to being kids again.

"That was fun," Kelly said.

I hadn't expected a deb to imitate a chicken. That would definitely make its way into my article. In spite of Kelly's perfect hair, I really liked her. "Any chance I could interview you for the school paper?"

"Allie's a good reporter," Sam added. "She wrote an article about Penny and me that will be in the next edition."

"Can't wait to read it," Kelly said, "but I don't have a horse, not even a dog. What would you write about me?"

"I don't know yet. Figuring it out is the fun part."

"Maybe you could interview me in a couple of months. I'm really busy with cheerleading practice and some stuff at home."

The way she said *stuff at home* caused my reporter's antenna to hum. Kelly sounded sad. "I'll buy you a cherry coke at Scott's Drug Store."

Kelly smiled. "You're determined. I like that."

Sam nodded her approval.

And that's how I landed an interview with the head deb.

Scott's Drug Store hadn't been updated since the 1950s. I guess the owners didn't have the money to fix it up. It was the kind of place that reminded me of *Happy Days* on TV. All we needed was the Fonz to punch the jukebox and yell, "Aaaaay." I sat in a red vinyl booth facing Kelly. We both ordered cherry cokes.

"Where did you move from?" she asked.

"New Jersey."

"That's a long way and this is officially the middle of nowhere. Why here?"

"My grandparents retired to Blowing Rock, and my mom wanted to live closer to them." I was surprised she was interested. "You ask as many questions as a reporter. If I tell Webb, he'll pester you into writing for the paper."

"Don't tell him," Kelly said. "Between cheerleading and fund-raising, I don't have time."

My reporter's antenna went up. "What kind of fund-raising?"

A waitress in a pink uniform served our Cokes. "Had a chance to look at the menu?"

We ordered some french fries, and I tried again. "What kind of fund-raising?"

"For St. Jude Children's Hospital." Kelly swirled the straw in her Coke. "My sister has leukemia. She's being treated at St. Jude's."

I should have known better, but I had expected Kelly's life to be as perfect as her hair. "I'm sorry about your sister."

"That's why I'm organizing a car wash and a bake sale. To raise money for research."

I started to get excited about the article. If it was good enough, maybe more kids would help with fund-raising. Maybe my story could make a difference. "Do you think your mom would give permission for us to print a photo of your sister?"

"Probably."

"Webb's expecting me to write about cheerleading, but I think fund-raising is more important."

"The cheerleaders are all working at the bake sale," Kelly said.

"They are? There's my title—'Cheering for a Cause'!"

"I like it," Kelly said, "but if you're going to write this story, you need to understand about Jenny's treatments."

I didn't want to hear about that. Since Eric died, I felt everybody else's sadness too, and it magnified mine.

"Jenny's weak," Kelly said. "She'll probably be in a wheelchair. She's lost all her hair, and she's so skinny. It makes her eyes look huge."

The more Kelly spoke, the sadder I became. That's the problem with a reporter's antenna: sometimes I discovered things it would be easier not to know.

Cheering for
a Cause

After my interview with Kelly, I walked home. Alone.
Everybody has a story, but I wished more of them
were happy ones. Kelly was afraid Jenny would die.
That made me think of Eric. He hadn't suffered like
Jenny, but at least Kelly would have time to say good-
bye. That's what bothered me the most. I didn't get
the chance to say good-bye.

Back in my room, I plopped down in front of the
typewriter. The words wouldn't come to me. I
wadded up yet another sheet of paper and lobbed it
at the overflowing wastebasket. Too depressed to

write, I stretched the phone cord from the hall to my room and called Sam instead. "Hi."

"Ribbit, ribbit," she answered. "You don't sound so good. What's wrong?"

I had only spoken one word, but Sam had tuned in to my mood. Between sniffles, I spilled the whole story, how talking to Kelly had reminded me of Eric. Sam didn't interrupt, not even once.

When I finished she said, "If you were like Kelly, and had the chance to talk to Eric again, what would you say to him?"

"I don't know for sure. I guess . . . I guess . . . I'd tell him I love him."

"Didn't he already know?"

That was a simple question, but it was profound, at least for me. I thought about cheering at Eric's baseball games. I remembered him saying, *Allison is my number one fan*. And Eric's last Christmas, though I hadn't known it would be his last, I'd made a scrapbook for him about his baseball season. "He knew."

"So why are you beating yourself up over something he already knew?"

A voice deep inside me answered. Eric had known how much I loved him. I had shown him in a hundred different ways. "Sam, you're right! He did know! Eric knew it all along."

"Of course he did. I know Melissa and Jonathan love me, even if they don't say it all the time."

Sam's words caused something important to happen: a piece of my broken heart clicked back into place.

The bake sale/car wash was held in the parking lot of the First United Methodist Church. Coach Murphy used her whistle to direct traffic. Reverend Walker led a special prayer service in the chapel.

"Hey," Kelly yelled from the bake sale booth. "Come and meet Jenny."

Jenny had Kelly's great smile. A red cowboy hat shaded her face and covered her head. I bent down so that I was level with her wheelchair. "Could I take your picture for the school paper?"

Jenny nodded.

While I snapped a couple of photos, she chattered away. "I like the chocolate cake the best, but the oatmeal cookies are good too, and the brownies are double fudge. Do you like double fudge?"

"Yes."

"How old are you, Jenny?"

"Six. How old are you?"

"Twelve."

"You're the same age as Kelly and Sam."

"You know Sam?"

"Of course I do, silly. She gave me the cowboy hat and brings Penny to visit me."

"She does, huh?" I'd watched Sam play with Jonathan, so I wasn't surprised. Sam loved kids.

I met Kelly and Jenny's mom next. Mrs. Hutton had the same tired, sad look as my own mom. I wished I could promise her things would get better, but I knew sometimes they get worse.

Mrs. Hutton signed a permission slip so that I could put Jenny's picture in the school paper. "Be sure and write how much we appreciate everyone showing up here," she said.

After that I took some photos of the car wash. Sam and Dwayne were scrubbing a brown farm truck that had seen better days. They looked like a couple of drowned rats. "What happened to you two?"

"Sam turned the hose on me," Dwayne said. He

dipped his rag in a bucket of soapy water and laughed. "And you know I couldn't let that slide."

Sam lifted the end of her shirt and wrung the water out. "Big D was working up a sweat. I had to cool him off!"

Watching Sam and Dwayne cheered me up a little, but Jenny's wheelchair and cowboy hat had made my heart hurt.

I slipped into the chapel just in time to hear the last words of Reverend Walker's prayer service. "Talk to God the same way you talk to your father. Tell him your troubles and ask for his help."

I wasn't speaking to my real father, but maybe God would listen to me. I asked for two miracles: for Jenny to get well, and for my parents to get back together again.

One True Way

Sam stretched across her bed and closed her eyes. "I'm tired. Washing cars is hard enough, but farm trucks caked with mud are a pain in the butt."

I curled up on the twin bed opposite Sam's with *Johnny Tremain*. "Do you believe in prayer?"

"What?" Sam's eyes blinked open. "Where'd that question come from?"

I told her about praying for Jenny and my parents at the prayer service.

"Sure, I believe in prayer. It's church I have a problem with."

"Why?"

"Start with the name One True Way. What if there isn't one? Most kids are whatever religion their parents are. I'd probably be Jewish or Muslim if that's the way I'd been raised."

"You probably would, but maybe not. I guess each person has to find their own true way."

"What's yours?" Sam asked.

Her question stopped me like a roadblock. Knowing what's true should have been easy, but it wasn't. I had to look deep inside. "I'm not sure when it comes to religion. Until Eric died, I hadn't given it much thought, but now I wonder. I wonder what happened to his soul, and if some part of him is still with me. Do you think I'm crazy?"

"Nope."

"A couple other things feel true too. Being a reporter and being with you."

A big smile spread across Sam's face. "Good answer. My church isn't true, at least not for me, but basketball, riding Penny, and being your best friend, all of those feel true."

She had said it! Sam had called me her best friend! I felt as warm and gooey inside as melted chocolate, but before I found the words to tell her, Sam's eyes drifted shut. "How about reading to me?" she asked.

My hands were trembling when I opened *Johnny*

Tremain, but soon I got lost in the story. The bedroom faded away and I was in Boston just before the Revolutionary War. I cringed when Johnny burned his hand on the furnace.

Sam's voice brought me back to the real world. "I like looking at you."

"What?"

"I like watching you read. When Mrs. Lapham sent for the midwife instead of the doctor, your face turned red."

A little self-conscious, I marked my place and closed the book. "Reading is an adventure. It's like I traveled to Boston without ever leaving your room."

Sam brushed her hair off her forehead and smiled. "Ready for a real adventure?"

"Maybe."

"Let's feed Penelope some carrots."

"That doesn't sound like such a big adventure."

"Just wait. You've never tried to hand-feed a horse before."

Sam and I walked through knee-high pasture grass that was starting to turn dry and brittle. She put her fingers to her lips and gave a shrill whistle. When she shook the brown paper bag she was carrying, Penny knew carrots were inside and came running.

"Our first lesson is called How to Feed a Horse and Keep Your Fingers," Sam said.

I stuck my hands deep into the front pockets of my jeans. "Maybe this isn't such a great idea."

"Oh, it's a great idea. Penelope has never bitten off anybody's fingers yet."

It was the *yet* that worried me.

"There's more than one way to feed a horse," Sam said. "Lots of people keep their palms flat, but if you get scared and move your hand, Penny could bite you by mistake."

I didn't want Penny to make a mistake. Not even a little one. "Okay, what's the best way?"

"Watch this." Sam wrapped her right fist around a carrot, leaving a few inches sticking out of the top. "Here you go, Penny."

Penelope used her lips and slid the carrot out of Sam's grip. "Good girl," Sam said. "See . . . I didn't jerk, or tease, or pull away. Penny wants the carrot, not my fingers."

"It'd be easier to throw the carrot on the ground."

"It would, but I want you to make friends with Penny. When the two of you get used to each other, riding will be as easy as walking."

I took a deep breath. My heart was beating like a snare drum, but I wrapped my fist around a carrot anyway. "I'm nervous."

Sam covered my fist with hers. "We'll do it together this time."

My fist tingled. I couldn't decide if it was because of Sam or Penelope. And if it was because of Sam, what did that mean?

Webster Wallace- Editor in Chief

Monday after school, I waited for Webb while Miss Holt graded papers. She had perfectly shaped oval nails. I'd been biting mine since Eric died, and I needed to stop.

Miss Holt looked up from her work and caught me staring at her. "How are you settling in here at Daniel Boone?" she asked.

"Good, mostly because of Sam."

"I enjoyed the article you wrote about her. It seems Sam's never met a stranger. She has a real knack for making friends."

"I wish I was like that."

Miss Holt shrugged. "Be who you are, Allie. You have different talents. Sam would struggle to write for the school paper the way you do." She tapped her red pen on the desk. "What would you like to write next?"

"That's easy. I'd like to interview as many seventh-grade students as I possibly can this year. It would be a good way for me to make friends."

Miss Holt let the idea slide in like Eric used to at home plate. "Most kids enjoy talking about themselves," she said, "and it would be interesting for teachers and administrators too. A way for us to learn even more about our students."

Webb interrupted us, hurrying in with his briefcase. "Sorry I'm late. I was talking to Mr. Dezern about the reign of Czar Nicholas II. He may teach U.S. History, but the man is a treasure trove of knowledge about Europe too."

I liked Webb a lot. He was the only kid I knew who carried a briefcase and used words like *treasure trove*. "Where's Dwayne?" I asked. It was funny how on my first day Webb said he normally required a writing sample. He'd made it sound like kids were lining up to write for the school paper. Instead, Dwayne and I made up his entire staff.

"Big D's at basketball practice. He's a man of many talents." Webb sat down and pushed his glasses up on his nose. "What have you got for me there, Allie?"

I passed him the article about Kelly Hutton and her sister. "Cheering for a Cause" had more depth than the article I'd written about Sam. I'd researched St. Jude and challenged kids to get involved.

"Incredible," Webb pronounced. He pushed his glasses up. "I'll donate part of my allowance, and I bet other kids will too. This article matters! I may have to change your byline to Allie Drake—Star Reporter."

I loved being called a star! Eric had been a star baseball player, and Sam had won trophies, but I'd never been a star before.

Miss Holt spoke up. "Allie would like to make this a regular column."

"Agreed," Webb said. "Allie, who would you like to feature next?"

"You."

"B-b-b-b . . . b-b-but why?" Webb sputtered. "I'm the editor in chief."

"You're also a unique character."

Webb agreed to the interview, and that's when my problems started.

Webb's mom was in England visiting relatives, so he had his dad call my mom and invite me for dinner. I wanted to see where Webb lived and figure out the answer to the burning question most of my readers were probably wondering about: why did he carry a briefcase?

On our walk to his house, Webb kept switching said briefcase from his right hand to his left. "What have you got in there?"

"I'd tell you, but then I'd have to kill you," Webb joked. "Books. I mostly carry around books."

"Why?"

"When my grandfather died, he left me his library and his briefcase. Gramps was my favorite relative." Webb gestured toward a house surrounded by a white picket fence. "Welcome to my humble abode."

I followed him through an arbor with climbing red roses to a hidden garden.

"You should see it in the spring when the phlox and hydrangeas are blooming," Webb said.

I couldn't picture him grubbing in the dirt. "You work in the garden?" I asked.

"I'm a gentleman farmer. We raise herbs and vegetables, and grow both perennial and annual flowers." He pointed toward a bed of purple blossoms. "Our fall pansies should last for a couple more weeks yet."

I ran over to a stone bench and sat down. The shrubs were planted around it like an outdoor room. It had a magical feeling. "Reminds me of *The Secret Garden*."

"I've read that book too," Webb said.

After I had thoroughly explored outside, Webb showed me his library, a dark-paneled room with bookshelves on all four walls. A biography of Winston Churchill lay on a table painted like a chessboard.

"Do you play chess?" Webb asked.

"No."

"What about Diplomacy?"

"What's that?"

"Only the best board game in the history of the world, but don't take my word for it. John F. Kennedy thought so too."

"John F. Kennedy, huh?" Webb had to be the smartest kid I'd ever met.

The Wallaces lived a lot more formally than Mom and me. Webb's dad had set the table with fine china and cloth napkins.

"I hope you like shepherd's pie," Webb said.

"I don't think I've ever had it before."

"The crust is made of mashed potatoes," Webb said. "Underneath is a stew of ground meat, onions, carrots, and peas."

It was delicious.

Webb's dad sipped red wine and asked so many questions I felt like a game show contestant.

Yes, my mom was a librarian.

No, I didn't think my dad would be moving to North Carolina.

Yes, I liked DB Middle School so far.

No, Webster hadn't told me he could play the tuba, but I would LOVE to hear him.

Webb groaned. "Do not, I repeat, do not mention the tuba in your article."

I offered to help with the dishes, but Mr. Wallace suggested we get started on our homework instead.

Back in the library, Webb and I sat across from each other at the chessboard table. I doodled in my notebook and jotted down random thoughts for my article. I wished Webb would play the tuba for me.

"Allie . . . would you . . ."

I looked up from my doodling and Webb was the color of a bright red geranium.

"What is it, Webb? Just spit it out."

"Would you go . . . would you go . . . to the Pioneer Days Celebration with me?"

"Uh . . . maybe. What is Pioneer Days?"

"A weekend that celebrates our town's history. It's sort of like a fair."

I liked Webb too much to hurt his feelings, and besides, I was curious. I'd never been on a date before. But mostly the reason I said yes was to earn the byline *Allie Drake—Star Reporter*. "If you'll play the tuba and let me write about it, then I'll go with you."

"Deal!" Webb shouted.

Allie Drake–
Confused Girl

On the ride home, I stared out the window into the darkness. *Allie Drake—Star Reporter* had become *Allie Drake—Confused Girl.*

"What are you thinking about?" Mom asked.

She kept her eyes on the road and her hands at ten and two on the steering wheel. Her counseling sessions with Reverend Walker were helping, but she still hated driving at night. "Nothing."

Mom stayed quiet. She knew I'd eventually get around to telling her what was on my mind. "Do you remember the first time you really liked a boy?"

"Yes."

Mom launched into a story about her first date. It happened a long, long time ago, just before the dinosaurs. "How'd you know if you liked him more than just a friend?"

Mom pulled into the driveway, but neither one of us got out of the car. "Well, I thought about him a lot. My heart beat faster every time I saw him, but mostly it was the way I felt when he held my hand. Sort of breathless."

I didn't feel any of those things about Webb. "Did you want him to kiss you?"

Mom rummaged in her pocketbook and divided a Snickers bar with me. "Yeah, kissing him was nice."

I had zero interest in kissing Webb. Back when we were a normal family, Dad always used to ask, *What's your gut telling you?* It was his way of reminding me that deep inside I already knew the answer.

"Honey, it's okay if you like boys."

"I know, but is it okay if I don't like them? That's what's worrying me."

Mom laughed. "That's okay too. You're young. There's plenty of time left to fall in love."

.   .   .

As soon as the light went out in Mom's room, I called Sam. I stretched the long cord from the hall to my bed and plopped down. "Hi, Sam."

"I was hoping it was you."

I felt a goofy smile spread across my face.

"How did dinner at Webb's house go?"

"It was . . . different."

Sam laughed. "Hanging out with Webb always is. Did he teach you to play Diplomacy?"

"Not exactly." I told her about Webb asking me to the Pioneer Days Celebration, and how I mostly said yes so that he'd play the tuba for me.

"Oh."

"What's wrong?"

"Nothing. Nothing's wrong. I just thought we'd be going to Pioneer Days together, but it's no big deal. I'll ask Phoebe."

Phoebe with the feathered red hair. I wished I hadn't told Webb yes. I wished it all the way down to my toes. "Sam, have you ever kissed a boy?"

"A couple times during Spin the Bottle."

"Did you like it?"

"Not really. I'd rather play basketball with boys than kiss them. Hey, I got a question. Are we still having lunch tomorrow?"

"Why wouldn't we be?"

"I thought maybe you'd want to eat with Webb."

Why did one date have to be such a big deal? "I'd rather have lunch with you." My voice sounded froggy.

"Ribbit, ribbit," Sam said. "Relax, Allie. I was just making sure."

After she hung up, I sat cradling the phone for a long time.

Phoebe Moore—
Crazy for Crochet

Webb started following me around like a lovesick puppy. My article "Webster Wallace for President" made it even worse. I guess he figured if I wrote such nice things about him that it must be love, or at least an extreme case of like. It wasn't.

On the way to the lunchroom, Sam snapped her fingers in front of my face. "Earth to Allie. I repeat . . . Earth to Allie."

"What?"

"I promised Phoebe we'd have lunch with her."

"Again? She sits at Webb's table."

Sam grinned. "It doesn't really matter where we sit. It's like a nursery rhyme. Everywhere that Allie goes, Webb is sure to follow."

It had been that way for the past three weeks. I thought about hiding out in the library, but it was pizza day, and I was hungry. If I had a magic wand, I'd break my date with Webb without hurting his feelings.

Sam took a seat beside Phoebe, and in less than five seconds, Webb moved to sit beside me. He reached into his lunch bag and pulled out a jelly doughnut. "Sweets for the sweet," he said.

I used to think the old-fashioned things he said were funny, but not anymore. He'd even ruined my taste for jelly doughnuts.

"Hey, Webb, how's your garden?" Sam asked.

They talked about getting a garden ready for the winter and playing Diplomacy. I ate my pizza in silence.

"I wanna braid Penny's mane for the Pioneer Days horse show," Sam said. "I'm gonna ride her in three events: Barrel Racing, Western Pleasure, and Egg and Spoon."

"What's Egg and Spoon?" I asked.

"Riders hold the reins in one hand and balance an egg in a spoon with the other," Sam said. "The announcer gives instructions like walk, trot, or stop. The rider who holds on to his egg the longest wins."

"Sam came in second last year," Webb said.

She pointed her index finger at him. "I'm gonna win this year. I've been practicing."

"I'll help you get Penny ready," Phoebe said. "I'm good at making braids."

Of course she was. Red was becoming my least favorite hair color. I was in such a bad mood that I didn't even like myself.

Sam made a face at me. "Why are you scowling?"

"Too much homework," I muttered.

Sam shrugged. "Gonna eat that doughnut?"

When I shook my head no, she split it with Phoebe.

I wanted to snatch the doughnut out of Phoebe's hand. That's what a terrible person I was turning into.

"Allie, who are you planning to interview next?" Webb asked.

I had a mouthful of pizza, and before I could spit out Dwayne Williams, Sam reached over and patted

Phoebe on the back. "Interview Phoebe. She's great at crocheting."

Crocheting? Who wanted to read about crocheting?

"That's an excellent idea," Webb agreed.

I was outnumbered and couldn't think of a way to say no without looking like a jerk. So much for freedom of the press.

Since Phoebe lived on Oak Street, same as me, we stopped to get my camera. I ran inside, and then we shuffled through fall leaves on the way to Phoebe's.

"I live with my grandmother," Phoebe said.

"Oh." I wondered why, but didn't ask. I understood about families who are different.

"My parents dumped me here," Phoebe said matter-of-factly, "but I'm happier with Grammy."

"Why?"

"Because it's predictable."

Most kids would have thought *predictable* meant *boring*, but not me. I missed knowing what days Eric had baseball practice and what time Dad was coming home for dinner.

As soon as Phoebe opened the door to her grammy's house, I smelled cinnamon and raisins.

"Fresh-baked cookies!" Phoebe said. "Grammy bakes for Scott's Drug Store, but there's always plenty left for my friends."

"Pheebs, I'm in the kitchen," a woman called.

With snowy white hair and silver-framed glasses, Phoebe's grammy looked like a storybook grandmother. "Sit, sit, girls. I have oatmeal-raisin cookies warm from the oven."

Phoebe's grandmother bustled around the kitchen pouring us glasses of milk and serving cookies on flowered plates. "Just call me Grammy, same as Phoebe. All her friends do."

I dipped a cookie into my milk while Phoebe answered questions about her day at school.

"I know your mother from the library," Grammy told me. "I read Harlequin Romance novels, and she orders them especially for me."

My mom was a master at matching the right books to the right readers. Maybe she could even find some Sam would like. I'd have to ask her.

After cookies, we went to Phoebe's room. Whoa! Every square inch was covered in crocheted teddy bears, hats, shawls, scarves, baby blankets, and other things too. "You could open up a store and sell this stuff. I'd call it Crazy for Crochet."

Phoebe laughed. "I give the shawls to Reverend Walker. She takes them to people who are sick."

"What about the little hats and baby blankets?"

"They're for preemies in the hospital."

No wonder Sam liked Phoebe. She was nice, and her grandmother made the best cookies on the planet. "How'd you get started crocheting?"

"Grammy taught me when I was in second grade. I was still living with my parents then, and when things got really bad, I'd lock myself in my room and crochet."

My parents yelled at each other a lot after Eric died, but I didn't tell her that. "Do you use pointy needles when you crochet?"

"No, those are for knitting." Phoebe reached into a basket filled with yarn and pulled out a thin metal rod with a hook on the end. "I use a crochet hook. Want to try?"

"I probably couldn't do it."

"Bet you could. We could start with something easy, like a friendship bracelet."

Phoebe fished an extra crochet hook out of her basket. We rocked in matching chairs, like two little old women.

"Watch me," Phoebe said. "You start by making a slipknot."

With her coaching, I made a friendship bracelet in about fifteen minutes. It was actually fun and relaxing. "I did it!"

"Told you," Phoebe said. "I'll give you some yarn and a hook to take home with you."

I snapped pictures of her wearing a crocheted hat and holding a blanket. I'd call this article "Crazy for Crochet." "Phoebe, why don't you start a crochet club? I'd help make baby hats and blankets, and I bet other kids would too."

"That's a good idea," Phoebe said. "I thought you were a sourpuss, but I like you, Allie Drake."

I liked her too. "I'm not really a sourpuss; I've just been in a bad mood lately."

"Why?"

The truth was I didn't like Phoebe sitting beside Sam at lunch, but I couldn't tell her that. She'd want to know why it mattered, and I didn't have a good answer. "Webb. He likes me more than I like him."

"Oh, that's too bad. When you crocheted the bracelet so large, I assumed it was for Webb."

I slid the bracelet up higher on my arm. I'd made it too big for me, but it'd be just right for Sam.

What Does the Bible Say?

On Saturday Mom dropped me off at Sam's house so that I could help her practice for the horse show. Sam climbed onto Penny's back, and I handed her a hard-boiled egg and a spoon. Once Sam started riding around the ring, I climbed to the top fence rail and sat down to watch. "Reverse direction and trot," I called.

Sam and Penny did as I instructed. "Lope," I yelled. They picked up speed. "And stop." The egg rolled off the spoon and plopped into the dirt.

Sam reined Penny in beside me. "How long?"

"Five minutes."

Sam shook her head. "Not good enough. I need to double that time if I'm gonna win."

I handed Sam another egg from the bucket, and she tried again. About an hour later, Sam led Penny over to me. "Want to ride her?"

"You mean right now?"

Sam nodded.

I jumped down from the fence and took a deep breath. "She looks so big."

"Nothing to be afraid of," Sam said.

Penny stood swatting flies with her tail while I listened to Sam's instructions. I placed the reins in my left hand and turned the stirrup toward me with my right one. I'd watched Sam a bunch of times, so I knew exactly what to do. The problem was getting my nerve up. I counted to myself, *One, two, three,* then stepped into the stirrup and swung my right leg over Penny's back.

"Good job," Sam said. "Remember how to use the reins to show Penny where you want her to go?"

"Yeah, I remember." My voice sounded scratchy.

"Ribbit, ribbit," Sam said.

I turned Penny to the right, and she walked around the ring. Even with a cool breeze, my palms were sweaty, and my underarms too. I tugged on the reins and reversed direction. Using my legs, I applied a little more pressure and lightly tapped Penny's belly with my heels. She went from a walk to a trot. My bottom bounced in the saddle.

Sam walked around the middle of the riding ring offering suggestions. "A little easier on the reins. You don't want to make her mouth sore. Not too fast, Allie. It's your first time."

Someday I wanted to leave the ring behind and gallop Penny across the pasture. It would be like flying. I just knew it.

When Sam called for a lunch break, I rode Penny toward the barn. Sam helped me unsaddle her and brush her coat. "I'm proud of you, Allie. You were great out there."

I was changing in all sorts of ways. The girl who had moved to North Carolina six weeks earlier would have never climbed on a horse's back. That girl would have been too afraid. I felt like Wonder Woman's kid sister!

I leaned against the fence while Sam turned Penny out to pasture. I watched while she closed the gate and walked toward me. Somehow in that moment I understood why I was jealous of Phoebe and irritated by poor Webb. I knew why I raced to answer the phone, and why I could hardly wait to see Sam each day. I liked her. I had a crush on her. It was, to borrow a word from Webb . . . stupendous!

"Why do you look so serious?" Sam asked.

I reached in my pocket and handed her the gold yarn friendship bracelet. "I made it out of school colors for you. Phoebe showed me how."

Sam slipped it onto her wrist. "See? A perfect fit."

I reached out and touched her arm just above the bracelet. "Do you like Phoebe more than me?"

"I like all my friends."

But that wasn't what I was asking.

Sam turned and stared directly into my eyes. "I don't like anybody as much as you."

My heart hammered so hard I could barely breathe.

Sam took my hand and put it over her heart. Hers was beating just as fast as mine.

The sky outside the barn door seemed bluer than blue. My hands were tingling, and I wanted to hug her, but I was afraid to.

"I've always liked girls," Sam said. "I've known

since second grade when I had a crush on Kelly Hutton."

I had never had a crush on another girl, or on a boy either, but I'd always felt different. I just hadn't known why.

Sam squeezed my hand, and her palm felt rougher than mine from farm chores and handling a basketball. "This has to be a secret," she said. "Nobody would understand."

My eyes filled like puddles in a rainstorm. The other kids would think we were freaks.

Sam reached up and brushed a tear from my cheek. "Don't cry, Allie."

"I don't care what the other kids think."

"Yeah you do," Sam said, "and I do too, but the biggest problem is my mom. She'd put us on the prayer list at One True Way and start quoting scripture."

"You think she'd actually embarrass us like that?"

Sam nodded.

"I don't think my parents would mind. My dad has a brother who's gay, and Mom is friends with Coach and Miss Holt."

"Maybe you're right, Allie, but my mom would try and keep us apart."

I leaned in closer to Sam so that our shoulders touched. I didn't believe like the people at One True Way, but I wondered what my own church had to say about kids like us. I needed to find out.

Sam and I had lunch in the kitchen. Over bowls of her mom's homemade chicken noodle soup, we snuck glances at each other. We smiled shy, sweet smiles, but I couldn't stop thinking about what other people would say if they knew.

When Mom came to pick me up, Mrs. Johnson invited her to stay for lunch. They had a friendly argument, with Mom insisting she couldn't impose, and Mrs. Johnson assuring her it would be a pleasure. Finally, the smell of homemade chicken soup was more than Mom could resist.

She sat down beside me and said, "I have a surprise for you girls. Murph and Franny have invited us to dinner tonight."

Mrs. Johnson clanged the metal soup pot with her ladle. "Didn't mean to make such a racket, but the girls shouldn't be spending time around women who live in sin. It's like that Anita Bryant says, 'Homosexuals cannot reproduce, so they must recruit.'"

Mom picked up her napkin and wiped her mouth a lot longer than necessary. "Franny and Murph would never behave in that manner. I'm going to be there, and Reverend Walker too. Surely you don't object to the girls enjoying a meal with neighbors."

Mrs. Johnson's lips puckered like a prune. "Samantha has to be up early for church. Maybe Allie should spend the night here and attend One True Way in the morning. A good sermon would help them more than anything."

"That's up to Allie," Mom said.

My eyes were drawn to Sam's like a magnet. Her jaw was clenched. I couldn't leave her alone with Mrs. Johnson—at least not today. "I want to stay here, Mom. Apologize to Murph and Miss Holt for me."

As soon as we finished our soup, Sam and I escaped to her bedroom. She paced around the room shaking her fist. "I told you. I told you how Mom is."

"She's wrong."

"How do you know?" Sam asked. She opened one of her dresser drawers and pulled out a Bible. "Have you ever read Leviticus 18:22 or Romans 1:26?"

It took me a couple of minutes to find the book of Leviticus. It said people like Sam and me were abominations. That means hateful and disgusting. Sam was the opposite of that. She liked everybody. She was kinder to her horse than most people were to each other. She gave piggyback rides to her brother, and every week she went to see a little girl dying of cancer. I closed the Bible. "I don't understand."

Sam's hands were still clenched. "Me either. When I was ten, I told our youth director how I felt about other girls. She said if I wanted to be saved and see the kingdom of heaven, I'd have to change."

"She meant well." That sounded like something my mom would say, but it was probably true.

"Whatever she meant, it didn't help."

I found out when Eric died that sometimes people say stupid things, like the people who say everything happens for a reason. I mean, c'mon, what good reason could God have for the death of a kid? "If Melissa would let me borrow her bike, we could ride into town and talk to Reverend Walker. She'd understand."

"I'm not sure that's such a good idea," Sam said.

But she followed me anyway.

Reverend Walker

The Methodist church was painted white, and its steeple rose high into the air. Sam and I parked our bikes and hurried around back to Reverend Walker's office. I took a deep breath and knocked on the door.

"Come in," Reverend Walker called. She sat behind a large desk, scribbling on a legal pad. Her Bible lay open in front of her. She pushed her reading glasses on top of her head and smiled. "Sam, are you selling candy?"

Sam shook her head. "No, not today, but I'll be back with pecan clusters next month."

Reverend Walker groaned and patted her stomach. "Have a seat, girls."

Sam and I pulled two wooden chairs closer to the

desk, but now that we were sitting in front of her, I didn't know how to begin.

"Will I be seeing you two later at Murph and Franny's?" Reverend Walker asked.

Sam looked down and scuffed her boot on the floor. "My mom won't let me go because . . . well, just because."

"Ah . . . now I understand why you're here."

We weren't being totally honest with Reverend Walker, but it was easier to talk about Coach and Miss Holt than ourselves. "Are they an abomination?" I blurted out.

"That's a strong word," Reverend Walker said. "For me the most important biblical passages are pertaining to Jesus. He never mentioned homosexuality, not even once."

"I didn't know that," Sam said.

Reverend Walker continued, "I try to love everyone that walks through our church door. People who feel judged leave."

"I don't think Coach and Miss Holt would be welcome at One True Way," Sam said.

Reverend Walker clasped her hands in front of her and leaned forward. "I'm sorry to hear that. I can't speak for another minister, but I will quote Romans 3:23. 'For all have sinned and fall short of the glory of God.' The Bible says *all*; it doesn't single anyone out."

"But is it a sin or not?" I persisted.

"My church says it is," Reverend Walker answered, "but my church also tells me to read the Bible and pray for discernment."

"What does that mean?" Sam asked.

"To pray and search your own hearts. Another of my favorite verses says, 'Seek and ye shall find; knock, and it shall be opened to you.'"

Sam and I would have to find our own answers. It was like hoping for a true/false quiz and being assigned an essay.

"Pray with me," Reverend Walker said. She bowed her head. "Gracious Lord, Sam and Allie are asking hard questions. Pour your wisdom upon them and guide their search for the truth. Amen."

On our way out the door, Reverend Walker added the most important thing. "Girls, I've searched my own heart, and I don't believe homosexuals are an abomination of any kind."

That one sentence made the whole trip worth it.

When Sam and I got back to her house, Jonathan came running. She swung him up into her arms. "What's going on, Jon Jon?"

"Pioneer Days!" he said. "I'm gonna wear a cowboy hat and boots."

Sam's mom had a pattern and a large piece of fabric spread across the kitchen table. "I'm sewing up a dress for Melissa. She's outgrown her old one."

The pattern was for a long dress and an apron. I had been so worried about going with Webb that I hadn't bought a costume yet.

Melissa opened the refrigerator and poured grape Kool-Aid for all of us. "Allie, want to borrow my dress from last year? I would offer it to Sam, but she always wears jeans."

When I said yes, Melissa whisked me away to her room faster than you can say Daniel Boone. Sam stayed behind to play with Jonathan.

"Allie, could I give you a makeover?" Melissa asked.

"I . . . I guess so. Do I look bad?"

"No, but I'm itching to trim your bangs and get them out of your eyes."

Melissa pushed me into a chair, draped a towel around my neck, and grabbed her scissors. "Don't worry. I cut my own hair all the time."

I took off my glasses and Melissa became a blur. As she snipped, soft blond hair rained down on my cheeks.

In no time at all, Melissa was finished with my bangs and searching through a basket of beauty products. She shook a tube of mascara. "Your eyes are hiding behind your glasses. A little mascara will make them pop."

As she used the mascara wand, I struggled to keep my eyes open. Next came blush and lip gloss.

After she finished working her makeup magic, Melissa handed me my glasses. "Go take a look."

I stood up and walked over to the mirror hanging above her chest of drawers. I looked brighter, like she'd taken a black-and-white photo of me and changed it into a colored one. I ducked my head, wondering what Sam would think.

Melissa rummaged in her closet, pulling out a blue gingham dress with a matching bonnet and a white pinafore. "I'll turn my back while you try it on."

I shimmied out of my shirt and jeans and pulled the blue dress over my head. Melissa buttoned it up the back for me. "Let's call Sam to take a look."

Sam tromped up the steps and down the hall. She leaned against the doorway, staring at me.

I smoothed the pinafore with shaky hands.

"You look great, Allie. As pretty as Penny when I get her ready for a horse show."

"What kind of compliment is that?" Melissa asked. "Who wants to be compared to a horse?"

I did. It was Sam's way of saying I looked beautiful.

"Do you know how to square dance?" Melissa asked. "All of the dancing at Pioneer Days is old-fashioned. It's nothing like *American Bandstand* or *Soul Train*."

Dancing made me think of Webb, and my voice came out all scratchy. "I don't know how."

"Ribbit, ribbit," Sam said. "Don't worry about it. I'll teach you."

"Melissa," Mrs. Johnson called, "I need to take your measurements."

I was alone with Sam.

"You look pretty, Allie." She grabbed my hand and pulled me down the hall to her room. "I want to dance with you." She shifted her weight from foot to foot.

Nervous, I thought. *Same as me.*

Sam flipped through a stack of albums. "Usually square dance music has a fiddle and a banjo. My dad will call the figures."

"What's that?"

"Instructions. Just pay attention and follow your partner. Webb's pretty good."

Webb. I didn't want to dance with him, even if he turned out to be the best square dancer in the whole county.

Sam played a fast fiddle tune and grabbed my hands. "Swing your partner 'round and 'round."

She had rhythm. Sam moved quick and graceful, just like on the basketball court. I stepped on her foot. "I'm not very good at this."

Sam didn't answer. *"Pick up your partner, and whirl her around."*

She lifted me off my feet as if I were no heavier than Jonathan.

"Stop worrying about looking dumb. Listen to

the words and have fun. *Ace of diamonds, jack of spades, meet your partner and promenade.*"

I quit worrying and started laughing.

Sam smiled. "Much better."

I was sorry when my lesson was over. I glanced down at my right hand. Dancing with Sam had turned my mood ring from brown to violet. I wondered if she knew what the colors stood for. Brown meant anxious, and violet meant happy. Dancing with Sam had made me happy.

Who's an Abomination?

When I woke up on Sunday morning, Sam was already dressed and sitting on the twin bed opposite mine. "Why are you wearing jeans?" I asked. "Aren't we going to church?"

Sam wrinkled her nose. "I'm not wearing a dress one minute longer than I have to." She reached into her pocket and pulled out a quarter. "See this? Every Sunday I use it to make holes in my panty hose during preaching. Mom never gets the message, though. She keeps buying new ones."

The hose themselves didn't matter, but how they

made Sam feel did. She felt ridiculous in hose and a skirt. "I'm sorry, Sam. I wish you could wear your jeans."

"Me too."

After I showered and put on borrowed church clothes, Sam knocked on the bathroom door. "Mom's got breakfast ready," she said.

We had pancakes and sausage patties. Instead of eating with us, Mrs. Johnson worked the griddle so the pancakes were served hot and golden brown.

"Jonathan, don't use all the syrup," she scolded. "Your pancakes are already floating in it."

Melissa reached over with a napkin and wiped his mouth.

Jonathan twisted his head. "Stop it!"

"He's gonna need a bath before church," Melissa said.

Mrs. Johnson stacked more pancakes onto a platter and carried it to the table. "Go ahead and finish them off. Dad had his breakfast earlier."

I helped myself to another pancake, and then Mrs. Johnson said, "I called Reverend Albert last night. I told him about Coach Murphy and Miss Holt.

They're setting a bad example, and it's my Christian duty to stop them."

My appetite disappeared.

Sam gripped the edge of the table with both hands. Her voice was clipped and angry. "Murph's my basketball coach. Why do you want to cause trouble for her?"

"Samantha Johnson, don't take that tone of voice with me."

"Murph is my friend. Leave her alone."

"She's not your friend; she's your teacher." Mrs. Johnson shook her spatula at Sam. "She's a pervert. Her lifestyle is disgusting. Why, she's an abomination, that's what she is!"

Sam stood up with clenched fists. "I hate that word. I. HATE. IT. Mom, don't you see what you're doing? You could cause Murph to lose her job. Or something even worse."

At that moment, all I wanted was to go home.

Jonathan's bottom lip trembled. Melissa stood and put her arm around him. "Stop it! You're scaring him."

All the fight went out of Sam when she looked at

Jonathan. She marched over to the kitchen door. "Allie, you should call your mom to come and pick you up."

"Where are you going?" I asked.

"Taking Penny for a ride."

"Sam, you head upstairs and get ready for church," Mrs. Johnson said.

Sam slammed the door instead.

Alone with Sam's family, I didn't know who to look at or what to say. "I need to use the phone," I mumbled and hurried to call Mom.

"Honey, is everything all right? You sound upset."

"Just come get me, okay?"

"You're scaring me. Are you in any kind of danger?"

"Mom, don't be ridiculous." I wanted to yell at her for jumping to conclusions, but what had happened to Eric stopped me. Sometimes the worst conclusion is the true one.

I stood shivering on the front porch, and Melissa waited with me. "It's chilly. Wouldn't you rather stay inside until your mom gets here?"

"No thanks. I'm fine."

"I'm sorry about what happened in there. My mom's afraid."

"Why?"

"The youth director at church told her some stuff, but it was no big deal. Sam was just a little kid then."

I looked up at the porch ceiling. "Sam trusted her. The youth director shouldn't have said anything."

"But Sam's not gay!" Melissa insisted. "If she were, I'd know."

Melissa was wrong, but I couldn't tell her. It was up to Sam. We stood shivering on the porch until Mom's Dodge Dart pulled up in a cloud of dust and leaves. "See you later. Ask Sam to call me after her ride."

While I climbed in, Mom drummed her fingers on the steering wheel. I had barely slammed the car door before she fired off a list of questions.

"What happened?

"Why are you so pale?"

"Where's Sam?"

I leaned my head back against the seat. "Sam had

a fight with her mom. She stormed out of the house and went for a ride on Penny."

"Oh. Is that all? Moms and daughters argue all the time. Once when I was your age—"

I held up my hand. "Don't, Mom. Just don't."

She didn't say another word on the ride home, but I knew, sooner or later, I'd have to tell her something. But what? I needed time to think.

A Good Daughter

I spent Sunday afternoon lying on my bed. I thought about the stuff Reverend Walker had told us. The words Sam's mom had used were stuck inside my head. *Abomination. Pervert.* The words even sounded ugly. When Mom knocked on my door, I turned my back to her.

She sat on the edge of the bed and tucked my hair behind my ear. "Talk to me, Allison. I hate seeing you unhappy."

"I don't have anything to say."

Mom rubbed my back in slow circles, just the way I liked. "You'll feel better if you do."

She waited.

I sealed my lips shut.

Mom rubbed my back some more.

Finally, I said, "Sam's mom called Reverend Albert from One True Way. She told him Coach and Miss Holt are a bad influence on kids."

"Ah." Mom sucked in her breath. "Then what happened?"

"Sam got upset and yelled at her mom. That's about it."

Mom gave my shoulder a gentle squeeze. "Try not to worry. I'll call Reverend Walker. Maybe she can talk to the pastor at One True Way and smooth things over. Hopefully, he's a reasonable man. Don't worry," Mom repeated.

But I did.

Sometime much later, the phone rang. "Allie," Mom called. "Have you heard from Sam?"

The tone of Mom's voice scared me. I hurried out of my room and down the hall. "No, I haven't talked to Sam since this morning."

Mom relayed the information and hung up the phone. "Sam hasn't come home from her ride."

It was already dark outside. Sam had to be cold and hungry. I started to shiver.

Mom put her arm around my shoulders and

steered me toward the kitchen. "There must have been even more to that argument than you told me." She filled the teakettle and put it on the stove. "Think, Allie. Where would Sam have gone?"

Of course there was more to the argument, but I didn't want to tell her. "Sam has lots of friends. She could be with any of them." I wished I could do the morning over and follow Sam to the barn. "Call Coach. She knows Sam better than anybody else. Even me."

While the water heated, Mom spoke with Coach Murphy. She grimaced when explaining why Sam ran away. Though it wasn't Coach's fault, what Mom said was bound to make her feel bad.

When the teakettle whistled, I poured hot water over our tea bags. Southerners drink iced tea, even when it's cold, but I hadn't gotten used to that. A cup of tea was more soothing.

Mom came back to the kitchen and sat across from me at the table. "Coach Murphy and Franny are going to look for Sam."

I could hardly breathe. I had hoped Coach would have heard from her. "Maybe we should look too."

"Murph asked us to stay put," Mom said. "There's a good chance Sam will show up here. Or maybe try to call you. I just don't understand why she would do this."

The words came tumbling out. "Because her mom called Coach an abomination. That's hurtful. It's . . . it's the same as calling Sam one."

Mom's mouth flew open wide. "Oh." She clutched her chest. "Are you telling me . . . ?"

I heard a roar. The blood rushed to my head too fast. "Yes."

"Sam hasn't tried to . . . to kiss you . . . has she?"

"No! I mean I've thought about it, but we've only held hands."

Mom shook her head back and forth. Hard. "You are way too young for that! Lots of times girls, and I suppose boys too, have intense feelings for each other, but it doesn't mean they're gay."

"If I'd told you I had a crush on Webb, would you have said I'm too young?"

Mom stared into her empty teacup.

"Well, would you?"

"No, probably not."

"Exactly. If I'm not too young to have feelings for a boy, then I'm not too young to have feelings for a girl."

"Maybe it's just a phase."

"I don't think so. I've thought about it a lot."

Mom cried. It started out silent, just tears snaking down her cheeks. "I'm sorry, Allie. I'm usually so tolerant, but somehow it's different when it's your own daughter. More personal, somehow."

"Are you disappointed in me?" Ribbit, ribbit.

"No, no, of course not."

But the tears and the look in her eyes told me a different story.

"It's . . . it's just that I don't want you to get hurt. I don't want you to be gossiped about, or called bad names, or maybe even assaulted by some terrible person."

Mom was trembling. It reminded me of the night Eric died. "Don't cry," I pleaded.

Mom reached for a napkin and wiped her face, but the tears kept pooling like a leaky faucet. I watched them. Drip. Drip. Drip.

"I failed Eric, and now I've failed you too," Mom whispered. "I should have kept you away from Sam and stopped this . . . this thing from happening."

Tears ran down my face to match Mom's. "You couldn't have stopped it." Honestly, I wasn't sure I could have stopped it either. I'd sworn to be a good daughter, to never cause Mom the kind of pain Eric's death had, but somehow I hadn't kept my promise.

Being Twelve

Our house was cold and lonely. Mom hadn't moved, but the distance from the kitchen table to the den couch seemed as far away as New Jersey. I wished she'd yell or scream or something. The silence was the worst. She was disappointed in me.

I dragged myself off the couch and peered out the window. My wristwatch said it was only seven thirty, but it felt like midnight. Where was Sam? I considered talking to Dad. Surely he would understand because of Uncle Jeffrey, but maybe not. I had seriously underestimated Mom's reaction. I called Reverend Walker instead.

It didn't take long for her to arrive and join Mom

at the kitchen table. I wanted to eavesdrop, but it would be humiliating to get caught. It already felt like I'd done something gross and awful just by liking Sam.

Mom's voice rose and fell, but Reverend Walker's was a slow, steady hum. I wished I were old enough to drive so I could look for Sam myself. Sometimes I hated being twelve. It meant depending on adults, and sometimes they only made things worse.

About an hour later, Coach and Miss Holt showed up at our front door. Alone. The haunted look in Coach's eyes got to me the most. "Allie, can we come in?"

A part of me wanted to slam the door in their faces. I was afraid of bad news. Afraid they'd tell me something that could never be fixed. Like the night Eric died.

I stepped aside and followed Coach and Miss Holt to the kitchen. While I refilled the teakettle, Coach said, "Sam spent the afternoon playing Diplomacy with Webb, but nobody knows where she went after that."

"Did you try Phoebe's?" I asked.

"Yes. She was at Phoebe's before Webb's, and had lunch with Dwayne Williams and his family."

"I bet she's at Kelly Hutton's house! Sometimes she goes to visit Jenny."

"I tried calling there and nobody answered. I even drove by, and the house was dark."

Sam was saying good-bye to all her friends. Once I had that thought, I knew it was true.

"The darkness is what worries me the most," Coach said. "I'm afraid of a driver not seeing Penelope until it's too late."

An image flashed through my mind of a car hitting Penny. I imagined Sam lying cold and still—like Eric. I pushed those thoughts away, because they hurt too much.

"Somebody should call and give Sam's parents an update," Coach said, "and it probably shouldn't be me."

Reverend Walker drummed her fingers on the kitchen table. "Murph, you *should* be the one who calls. Mrs. Johnson needs to know how much you care about Sam."

Coach's side of the conversation drifted from the

hall to the kitchen. She remained calm and professional, recounting all the places she'd looked for Sam. She asked if Mrs. Johnson knew of other places Sam might be.

Mom looked across the table at me. "I love you, Allie."

I was too choked up to answer, but managed a nod. Deep down I'd known Mom wouldn't stop loving me, but was she still proud of me? Or would there always be this empty space between us?

A few minutes later, Coach came back to the kitchen. She leaned against the counter and crossed her arms. "Mr. Johnson is out on his tractor. He's driving through the fields and pastures. Places a car can't go."

"How's Mrs. Johnson holding up?" Reverend Walker asked.

"She's scared," Coach said. "She loves Sam. There's no doubt about that." Coach paced from one end of the kitchen to the other. "I can't sit here and do nothing. I'm gonna drive around back roads and then through town. Sam's gotta be out there somewhere."

I was on my feet and beat Coach to the front door. "I'm going too!"

Skeletons

Coach Murphy's car crept down country roads with no streetlights. I peered out the passenger side window at bare fields and tree limbs that looked like skeletons. There was hardly any traffic and no sign of Sam or Penelope.

"I blame myself for this," Coach said.

"Why?"

Coach stared out the windshield into the darkness. "Because I didn't keep a professional distance between myself and Sam. I thought she needed somebody who understood."

I remembered Sam saying she had asked Coach a hard question and Coach had told her the truth.

"Sam told me when she first met you, she knew you were like her."

"That's what is bothering me," Coach said. "I felt really desperate a few times when I was Sam's age. Like nobody would ever understand me. You don't think she'd try to hurt herself, do you, Allie?"

"You mean on purpose?"

"Yes, on purpose."

Her question made tears well up in my eyes. "I think she ran away." I couldn't stand to think of the alternative.

"Then we'll just have to keep looking until we find her."

The longer we drove without spotting Sam, the more anxious I became. All of the winding roads started to look the same.

"Don't cry, Allie."

I brushed away tears with my coat sleeve. "It's like the night Eric died. He didn't come home. Dad drove around looking for him. Mom started calling hospitals. Finally, a policeman showed up at our door."

"Bad memories give me the same feelings as these

bare tree limbs," Coach said. "Lonely. Would you mind if I prayed for Sam?"

Coach talked to God as if he were her best friend. "We need some help here. I don't know where else to look. Sam is a special person. Of course you already know that, but we're asking you to watch over her."

A warm feeling wrapped its way around my heart. "Coach, I like Sam. I mean . . . I really like her."

"I'm not surprised."

"You're not?"

"No. I first suspected the night Franny and I had dinner at your house. When you said Sam was the most interesting person you'd ever met, your cheeks were the same color as Franny's summer roses."

"Mom cried when I told her."

"Moms do that. Give her time. She'll come around."

"What about Sam's mom?"

Coach shook her head. "Sam's mom believes in the teaching at One True Way. She thinks Sam's feelings are sinful. I was raised in a home like that. It took me years to get past it."

I was grateful my church had a gentler way of interpreting the Bible than Sam's. My mom was struggling, but at least she wouldn't threaten me with hell.

Coach turned the car around in a gravel driveway and headed back toward town. The narrow road grew wider and turned into Main Street. Coach made a right onto Apple Avenue. "I'm gonna swing by my house and use the telephone. Maybe somebody's heard from Sam."

I was out of ideas and started to silently pray.

The driveway dipped and the car's headlights flashed against Coach's front porch. "Look!" I screamed. "Look!"

It was Sam.

How Do You Mend a Broken Heart?

Sam was sitting on the front porch steps. Coach barely had time to stop the car before I was out and running. "Where have you been?" I cried. "Where's Penny?"

Sam's teeth were chattering.

Coach unlocked the front door. "Let's go inside and get warmed up."

While Coach made hot chocolate, I sat beside Sam at the kitchen table, waiting to hear what had happened.

Finally, she said, "Penny's at the vet's. A

barbed-wire fence was down and she got tangled up and cut her leg."

"Will she be okay?"

"The vet thinks so. I'll get Dad to take the trailer and pick her up tomorrow."

"Your parents are worried," Coach said. "You have to call and let them know you're okay."

Sam scowled. "I was running away, but Penny got hurt."

I reached under the table for Sam's hand and held on tight.

"You and Penny are safe now," Coach said. "That's what counts."

Unlike at my house, Coach's phone hung on the kitchen wall. She handed the receiver to Sam. "Allie and I will be waiting for you in the den."

I knew giving Sam privacy was the right thing to do, but I hated leaving her alone. Mrs. Johnson might say something to hurt Sam even more. She wouldn't mean to. It was like Coach said: she only wanted what was best for Sam, but she didn't understand. Not one bit.

Sam's eyes were red when she joined Coach and

me in the den. "My dad will be here in about fifteen minutes."

Coach picked up our empty mugs. "I'll wash these and give the two of you a chance to talk."

Sam sat down beside me on the couch. "I'm gonna quit basketball," she said.

"But why?"

"So Mom will leave Coach alone. We made a deal."

I remembered Coach saying Sam had the potential to be a standout in high school. "But you love basketball, and you're so good at it."

Sam shrugged. "I don't know what else to do. But I'm pretty athletic. I can pick up a different sport."

Then I told Sam about Mom. How she was disappointed. About Mom's fears for me and how she cried. "I need to give her some time to accept that I'm not exactly the daughter she hoped for."

"Guess that means we won't be seeing each other outside of school," Sam said.

"Yeah, I don't see how that would work." Ribbit, ribbit.

Sam reached for my hand. "Ribbit, ribbit," she answered.

We sat with tears running down our cheeks until her dad arrived. Sam got up and trudged over to the door. "'Bye, Allie. I'll miss you."

"I'll miss you even more."

Allie Drake-
Square Dancer

The news that Sam had quit the basketball team spread faster than the flu. I sat across the lunch table from Webb, staring down at a plateful of pinto beans. I hadn't gotten used to pintos or collard greens. I wished I'd packed my lunch.

"Is it true about Sam quitting the basketball team?" he demanded.

"Yeah, it's true."

Webb's eyes widened, and he sucked in his cheeks. It reminded me of the way he looked when he played the tuba. "You've got to write that story!"

he said. "The whole school is wondering what happened."

"No."

"No! Why not? This is big news. All the kids would read that article!"

"And that's why I won't write it." I told him the story Sam and I had agreed on. "It's embarrassing, but she has to get her grades up."

"Oh." Webb munched on a carrot stick. "That makes sense. Sam's never done well in English, or history either."

I looked over Webb's shoulder, scanning the lunch tables to see which kid was lucky enough to be with Sam. She was sitting with Big D. I watched her hands move, shooting a pretend basketball. Sam and Dwayne were always doing that. They were probably talking college sports again.

Webb snapped his fingers to get my attention. "Did you hear me?"

"Ummm, yeah. Pioneer Days. You said something about Pioneer Days."

"We should get together and practice square dancing," Webb repeated.

At the mention of square dancing, my hands and waist tingled. I remembered that day in Sam's room. *Pick up your partner, and whirl her around.* I could almost feel Sam lifting me off my feet. I wished I could dance with her again.

"So do you want to come over to my house?" Webb asked.

I took a sip of chocolate milk and tried to think of a good excuse to say no. There wasn't one. "Why don't you come to my house instead?" Not that I wanted to spend more time with Webb, but it would make Mom happy.

One of the things I missed most about New Jersey was good Italian food. Mom knew that, and all week she'd made Italian—eggplant parmesan, meatball subs—and for my square dancing date, she'd saved her specialty, spaghetti Bolognese.

On Friday, Webb walked me home from school. "You've been different this week," he said. "Sort of quiet and sad."

I kicked at fall leaves with my sneaker. "I feel bad about Sam quitting the basketball team. That's all."

"I feel bad too," Webb said. "But you're acting as if it happened to you."

I didn't know how to answer that. I couldn't tell him I was unhappy because Sam was unhappy, and she was unhappy because of me.

I unlocked the front door, and a meat sauce aroma wafted over us.

Webb closed his eyes and inhaled. "Garlic and fresh basil. Two of the most stupendous smells on earth!"

Mom peeked around the kitchen corner. She smiled, which meant she was glad to see me with Webb. I could read her like a favorite book. "You have a good nose for herbs," she said.

Webb launched into a description of his garden. I hoped he'd talk a long time so we could skip the dancing.

"I moved the coffee table so you can practice in the den," Mom said, "and I brought a couple of square dancing albums home from the library."

She had put a lot more effort into this date than I had. I led Webb to the den and put on some music.

Webb held out his hand and I took it. "Just follow my lead, Allie. I love to dance."

Sam was right. Webb was an excellent dancer. He picked me up and whirled me around, but there was no tingle when he touched me. No spark. No racing heart. He wasn't Sam.

"You're doing great!" Webb said. "Nobody would ever guess you're new at this."

I was doing great because I wasn't nervous about dancing with him. It made a difference.

Webb smiled at me. He was smart, and kind, and funny. It would be easier for me, and better for Mom, if I liked him instead of Sam. I needed to think a lot more about that.

Living a Lie

I didn't have any plans on Saturday. Feeling a little bored and lonely, I rode my bike to Reverend Walker's office. My life was such a mess that I needed help making sense of it.

I found her outside, filling up a bird feeder that hung from a maple tree. "Nice to see you, Allie. I was just about to make some Russian tea."

I followed Reverend Walker inside and cuddled up in a floral armchair. She poured hot water into two mugs and added the Russian tea mix. It smelled like fall: oranges, cinnamon, and cloves.

"Growing up is awfully confusing, isn't it?" Reverend Walker said.

It was an open-ended question, the kind my teachers often asked. It invited me to tell everything or only a little bit. I only meant to tell a little, but once I got started, the words came pouring out. How I'd always felt different. I explained why I'd thought Mom would understand. How she loved Uncle Jeffrey and was friends with Coach and Miss Holt. I told her how we'd all let Mom down: first Eric, then Dad, and now me. I confessed that going to Pioneer Days with Webb felt like a lie, but I didn't want to hurt his feelings, and it seemed to make Mom happy.

"I don't believe God wants you to live a lie, Allie."

"But what about those Bible verses? Sam's mom thinks people like us are going to hell."

"Consider the time period the Bible was written in. Put it into cultural context. First Corinthians 14:35 says it's shameful for a woman to speak in church. Can you imagine? And there are over two hundred verses dealing with slavery, but those verses don't apply to our lives today. Maybe the same could be said for the Bible's stance on homosexuality."

"I wish Mrs. Johnson could have heard the way Coach prayed for help finding Sam. She believes in God."

"I know," Reverend Walker said. "Murph is a wonderful person."

"What worries me the most is hurting Mom."

Reverend Walker gave me that beautiful smile of hers. "Your mom's afraid you'll be the one who gets hurt, but give her time to adjust. She loves you too much not to."

"Do you think I could be the one to adjust? Webb came over for dinner last night, and it made Mom so happy. If I could just like him instead of Sam, it would be a lot easier. When we were square dancing, I wondered how to change my feelings. Do you think I could?"

"Only you know the answer to that, Allie. There's no reason to rush. Take your time and decide what's right for you."

I finished my tea and placed the mug on her desk. "Thanks for listening."

"My pleasure. That's what I'm here for, but did I help you at all?"

"Yeah, talking helps, and I think you're right. There's no rush, but I'm the only one who can decide."

. . .

When I got back home, Mom was reading in the den. She held up her book. "This is *Roots* by Alex Haley. It's a fascinating read."

"What's it about?"

"The history of a slave family."

I loved almost any book with history in it. "Maybe I'll read it when you're finished." Mom didn't censor my reading. She was good about that.

"Where'd you bike to?"

"Church. Went to see Reverend Walker."

Mom used a bookmark and closed *Roots*. "I didn't handle this thing between you and Sam very well. I know that."

"There's not really a thing, Mom. I just realized I like her. I'm sorry it makes you unhappy. I'd change if I knew how."

"You're so young," Mom said, "and people can be so cruel. I want to protect you."

"I know."

"This could just be a phase," Mom said. "Why don't we give it a few months and then see how you feel?"

Mom didn't think I was old enough to know my own feelings. Saying it was just a phase irritated me, but I was the one who had decided not to rush things. "Okay, we'll wait and see, and, Mom, try not to worry so much."

Reverend Walker had said God didn't want me to live a lie, but that seemed better than hurting the person I loved most.

Big D and Me

I was late for Monday's newspaper staff meeting. Miss Holt, Webb, and Dwayne were all waiting for me.

"Sorry. I forgot to set my alarm clock." That seemed like a good excuse. The truth was I'd stayed in bed to avoid Mom.

Webb pulled out a typed agenda. The first item brought tears to my eyes. He'd gone behind my back and had Dwayne write about why Sam had quit the basketball team.

"Sam's gonna get some tutoring and spend more time studying," Big D said. "That way she can play in high school, when it really counts toward college."

Miss Holt chipped the polish from one of her

fingernails with her thumb. We both knew the real reason.

"Allie, which seventh grader do you want to interview next?" Webb asked.

"If you print that story about Sam, there won't be another interview. I'll quit."

"But it's my . . . my decision," Webb sputtered.

"It's an invasion of Sam's privacy," I countered.

Webb squinted at me through his glasses, letting me know he was irritated. The feeling was mutual. I squinted back.

Webb turned to Miss Holt. "We've reached an impasse. It's up to you."

Miss Holt rubbed her forehead and took a minute before answering. "I didn't step in initially because I wanted you to solve this problem by yourselves. Allie's right. This would be an invasion of privacy. I know real newspapers do that, but a school newspaper has a higher purpose, to foster community and highlight the accomplishments of its students, doesn't it?"

Webb's face flushed. "I didn't think of it like that. I'm sorry."

"Apology accepted," Miss Holt said.

We sat silent as statues until Dwayne jumped in. "Now that we're scrapping my story about Sam, we need a new article. How about Allie and I interview each other? We'll call it 'Dueling Reporters.'"

I was still irritated at Dwayne for writing the article in the first place, but he had the nicest smile. It was impossible to stay mad at him.

Miss Holt clasped her hands together, leaning toward me. "It'd be something new and interesting for our readers, and for you too, Allie. What do you say?"

I said okay. Saying no would have just caused a big stink. I spent the rest of the meeting daydreaming about Sam. We climbed on Penelope and rode far, far away. I wished the dream could come true.

Big D and I met after school in the library. The location was his idea. I would have rather gone to Scott's Drug Store for a cherry coke.

We opened our notebooks and stared at each other. We'd never really talked without Sam or Webb around. Normally, I would have made a list of questions, but it hadn't seemed worth the effort.

"How do you like DB so far?" Dwayne asked.

I shrugged. "Good."

Dwayne put his elbows on the table. "One- or two-word answers will make a mighty boring interview."

"Sorry."

"Maybe I didn't ask the right question. What I'd really like to know is why you went from happy to sad."

"It's a long story."

"We've got an hour before Mrs. Smitherman closes the library."

There was no easy way to explain. "The short answer is my brother died. That changed everything. My mom's sad, and she thinks I'm spending too much time with Sam."

Dwayne nodded. "Thought it had something to do with Sam." He scrunched his forehead so that it wrinkled like an old man's. "I watch people. Bet you do too, since you like to write."

"I do it all the time."

"And what I noticed," Dwayne said, "is your eyes shine whenever Sam is around."

"It's that obvious, huh?"

"It is to me."

We sat there awkward and silent. Finally, I said,

"We'd better get started on 'Dueling Reporters.' What do you want to be when you grow up?"

Dwayne told me how he hoped to someday go to the University of North Carolina and play for Coach Smith. "They've got a good journalism program too. What about you?"

"A reporter, same as you."

"Why'd you ask me about the future?" Dwayne said. "You didn't do that in any of your other interviews."

I didn't want to admit that talking about the future meant I could avoid talking about the present. "I don't know. That's just what happened."

As we were packing up our notebooks, Dwayne said, "You've got good taste in friends. Sam is about my favorite person around here."

"Mine too."

"Then tell your mom that," Dwayne said. "Stand up to her the way you stood up to Webb. That was something!"

I felt a smile spread across my face. "Maybe you're right. I need to speak up more!"

X-ray Vision

I headed out the main entrance to DB and there stood Sam, with her back to me. Her hands were shoved in her pockets, and her shoulders were hunched against the wind. I thought about walking away, but I couldn't stop staring at her. "Sam?" Ribbit, ribbit.

She looked over her shoulder. "Ribbit, ribbit."

"I stayed after school to interview Dwayne for the newspaper. What about you?"

"It's kind of pathetic."

"Tell me anyway."

"I hid behind the locker room door and watched basketball practice through the crack."

"That's not pathetic. That's sad."

"Don't you cry on me, Allie Drake."

"I can't help it. I miss you."

"I know, but your mom's been through a lot. Hanging around me will just make her sad."

"How are things going with your family?"

"They're still pretending I'm just a tomboy."

Sam's dad pulled up in his pickup truck. He was waiting, but we kept standing there. It was hard to say good-bye.

Mr. Johnson tapped his horn a couple times. "I gotta go," Sam said. "Don't look like that. Reminds me of a lost puppy."

But all I could think about was Sam watching basketball practice through a crack in the door. It was the most unfair thing I'd ever heard of. "Talk to your mom again about the basketball team. Maybe she'll change her mind."

Sam shook her head. "Talking wouldn't do any good." And then she turned away from me and walked toward the truck. "See ya around," she called over her shoulder.

My throat was too tight to answer her.

Mom made meat loaf and mashed potatoes for dinner. I took a couple bites, but mostly I used my fork to create mountain peaks with the potatoes.

"Allie, stop playing with your food and eat."

"I'm not hungry."

Mom sighed. "We agreed your feelings for Sam might be just a phase. Can't you at least make an effort?"

"Sam quit the basketball team."

"But she's a star player," Mom said. "Why did she quit?"

"So her mom wouldn't cause trouble for Coach. They made a deal."

Mom blotted her lips with a napkin. "I'm sorry about that, Allie. It seems awfully unfair."

"Sam stayed after school today and hid behind the locker room door. She watched basketball practice through the crack."

"Maybe Reverend Walker could talk to Mrs. Johnson. It's a shame what she's doing."

I stared at Mom as if I had Superman's X-ray vision.

"I get it," Mom said. "You think I'm as bad as Mrs. Johnson."

Dwayne had said I needed to stand up to Mom. I kept staring. She was the first to look away.

Sweet Melissa

Melissa called just before bedtime. I was surprised, and a little nervous too. Why would Sam's sister call me?

"Allie, you forgot to take the costume for Pioneer Days home with you."

"What?" Pioneer Days was the furthest thing from my mind, as far away as another galaxy.

"You left early that Sunday morning, and neither one of us remembered."

That Sunday morning had been the end of my friendship with Sam. I had replayed that day about a million times. Like if I thought about it long enough, I could go back and change the ending. "Yeah, to tell you the truth, I've been trying to forget about Pioneer Days because . . . never mind, it's a long story."

Melissa sucked in her breath. "I could stop by after school tomorrow and drop it off."

"You want to come here?"

"Yes." Melissa spoke softly, almost a whisper. "I need to talk to you."

Then it was my turn to breathe deeply. "Is it Sam? Is she okay?"

"Ummm . . . not really, but we should talk in person."

I wouldn't be able to sleep, or even think, until I heard what Melissa had to say. "Does Sam know you called me?"

I heard Mrs. Johnson in the background. "Melissa, are you tying up the phone again? Heaven forbid somebody tried to get through with a real emergency."

"Give me another minute," Melissa said. "Thanks for going over that algebra problem with me. It really helped."

I didn't know much about algebra, but I understood what had just happened. Melissa was keeping a secret from Mrs. Johnson.

I didn't blame her one bit.

Somehow I made it through the night and the next day. I went to my classes, but the lessons didn't sink in. I said hi to anyone who called my name, but it was an automatic response. I was a zombie.

After school, I hurried down Oak Street. Phoebe ran through piles of leaves to catch up with me. "Grammy's baking cookies again. Want to go home with me?"

"Not today. Melissa is dropping off my costume for Pioneer Days."

"Can I stop and see it?"

"NO!"

"I thought we were friends," Phoebe said. "You don't have to yell."

"Sorry. Sometimes friends yell."

"I hate it," Phoebe said. "My parents yelled all the time."

"Sorry," I repeated. "I need to talk to Melissa by myself. That's all."

"Is it about Sam? She quit practicing for the horse show and told me not to bother with braiding Penny's mane."

Sam was miserable too. I wished I knew how to fix it for both of us. "Bring your ribbons to Pioneer Days anyway. I bet Sam will change her mind."

"I hope so. She hasn't been the same since she quit the basketball team."

"I know. That's why I need to talk to Melissa alone. Maybe I can figure out a way to help."

While Phoebe and I said our good-byes, Melissa waited for me on the front porch. Mom's car wasn't in the driveway, which meant she was still at the library. Perfect.

I offered Melissa a snack, but she turned it down. She thrust a brown paper grocery bag into my hands. "The costume is in there."

I put the bag on the coffee table. "Want to hang out in here or in my room?"

"Here's fine." Melissa sat down and hid her face in her hands. "Sam told me."

I had to be careful. "Told you what?"

"All of it. That she's gay."

"Oh. I . . . don't know what to say."

"She told me about having a crush on Kelly Hutton when she was in second grade."

"She told me that too."

"I'm so mixed up. It feels like I don't know Sam at all."

"Sam's the same person she always was. She likes basketball and horses and loves little kids."

"Yeah, but I live with her. She's my sister. How could I not know something this important?"

Melissa was struggling, same as Mom. Why did it have to be such a big deal?

"It's just hard to accept. That's all."

"It had to be even harder for Sam to tell you." I remembered Mom's reaction and shuddered. I'd probably never forget how alone I'd felt that night.

"I asked Sam if she needed counseling, but I think after talking to the youth leader at church, she's done with that."

"What else did you say to her?"

"I promised that I wouldn't tell Mom or Dad. Both of us agree they couldn't handle it."

"I think you're right."

"The whole thing makes me want to cry," Melissa said. "I want Sam to be happy, but I don't know how to help her."

I knew what Sam needed from Melissa, because it

was what I needed from Mom. "Don't judge her. Don't make her feel like a freak. What she needs is to know you love her, and that you're still proud she's your sister."

"You think it's that simple?"

I brushed away stupid tears. "Yeah, it's that simple."

Melissa brushed away tears of her own. "Thanks, Allie. I'm gonna do all the things you said."

I had found a way to help Sam, or at least a way for Melissa to help her, but it really made me miss Eric. Siblings usually understand, even when your parents don't.

Melting an Iceberg

When Mom got home from the library, I was lying on the couch thinking about Melissa's visit.

"What's in the brown paper bag?" she asked.

"My costume for Pioneer Days."

Mom stopped unbuttoning her coat. Her fingers wrapped around the second button. "Did Sam bring it?"

I understood what she didn't say. She didn't want me to be alone with Sam. "Melissa brought the costume. She was by herself."

Mom's breath came out in a relieved whoosh, and she finished unbuttoning her coat. "Put the costume on. You can model it while I make dinner."

"It's nothing special."

"Put it on," Mom insisted.

"Okay, okay. I will." It was easier to do it her way than to argue.

While I got dressed, the phone rang. I put my ear against the bedroom door. It was Dad. I could tell by the tone of Mom's voice. She sounded overly polite and extra cheerful.

"I'm glad you called. How are you doing?"

I didn't understand how she could cut him so much slack. He had walked out on us. End. Of. Story.

Mom answered questions about her work in the library. She told him both her parents were doing well.

Finally, they got around to discussing me. "Things are about the same," Mom said. "Allie is unhappy, and she's blaming me for her misery."

I couldn't help but blame her. My crush on Sam should have been fun and exciting, but she had ruined the whole experience, with some help from Sam's mom.

"That's a wonderful idea," Mom said. "I could use the help." She paused, and I wondered what Dad was saying on the other end of the line. "John, there's no need for you to get a hotel. The house Allie and I are renting has a guest room."

Here. Dad was coming here. Maybe now he and Mom would finally get back together!

A couple days later, Dad was waiting for me when I got home from school. "Hi, Allison."

"Hi." I wanted to hug him, but I didn't. "Don't call me Allison. It's Allie now."

"Still mad at me, huh?"

I shrugged.

"Let's take a walk," Dad suggested. "You can show me the town."

"It's small. Not much to see."

Dad ignored my attitude. "We should leave a note for your mom." He walked into the kitchen and rummaged through the drawers.

"Just write it on the blackboard over by the cabinets."

I waited while Dad zipped up his coat, and then we were on our way. I acted like a polite tour guide, pointing out all the places that were important to Mom and me: Daniel Boone Middle School, the Methodist church, and the library. I lingered in front of Scott's Drug Store. "Can we get a cherry coke?"

"Sure, that sounds good. I know they're your favorite."

Dad took his time checking out the red vinyl seats and looking at the menu. "This place is a real throwback to the fifties. How about french fries?"

"Okay."

Dad reached into his pocket for a couple of quarters. "Want to play some music on the jukebox?"

I was glad for a reason to leave the table. I played "All I Have to Do Is Dream" by the Everly Brothers. It was Mom and Dad's favorite song from when they were in college.

"Ouch," Dad said. "That one brings back good memories."

That's exactly what I'd intended. I crossed my fingers.

Slurping our Cokes was easier than talking to each other. I wished the iceberg between us could melt as fast as the ice in my glass.

Dad finished his Coke and fished out a maraschino cherry with his straw. "I've been angry . . . and . . . and depressed since Eric died. I won't make excuses, but somehow I took it out on your mom."

I stared down into my glass. "Mom wasn't always nice to you either."

"No. No, she wasn't."

"Are you two getting back together?" My words were rushed, quick and hopeful. We could never have Eric back, but the rest of us could still be a family.

Dad shook his head and looked away from me. "I do have some good news, though. At least I hope you'll think it's good."

I stared at him and waited. Anything he said would be short of what I really wanted.

"I got a job transfer. My new sales territory will be the Southeast. I'm looking for a place nearby so I can spend more time with you."

"But what about Mom?"

Dad sighed. "It was a joint decision, Allie. We're better off apart, but you need us both."

"I need you living together in the same house."

Dad shook his head. "What you really want is the life we had before Eric died. Honey, no matter how hard we try, neither your mom nor I can give that back to you."

I knew he was right, but it was so hard to let my dreams go.

Dad reached for a napkin and wiped his watery eyes. "Remember how it was toward the end between your mom and me? Think about the fights, the crying and yelling."

I didn't want to go through that again. Nobody would.

The waitress bustled over and slid a platter of french fries between us. I dunked a couple of them in ketchup and thought about the stuff Dad had said. His knee was jerking under the table. I guess he was anxious too.

"I love you, Allie. More than anything."

Dad wouldn't be going to all this trouble if I didn't matter to him.

"Well, what do you think?" he asked nervously.

"The french fries are delicious."

Dad grinned and pointed one at me. "I mean about my move."

I knew what he meant. "It's not as perfect as if you lived with Mom and me, but it's still good."

"That sounds like my girl," Dad said. "I've missed her."

That me had disappeared the night Eric died. I had missed her too.

Dad Gets It Right

Mom made Dad's favorites for dinner. We had a pot roast cooked with potatoes, carrots, and thick brown gravy. Mom had fixed herself up too. I could tell she'd washed her hair and freshened her makeup.

"I've asked around," Mom said, "and Janet Moore has a garage apartment that might work for you."

"Phoebe's grandmother?" I asked.

"Yes," Mom said. "Phoebe's grandmother, baker of homemade cookies and reader of romance novels."

Dad grinned. "I'm only interested in the cookies."

Mom smiled back at him. "That's good. Mrs. Moore is about twenty years too old for you."

Dad had seconds on the pot roast. "Sure you don't mind me staying until I find a place?"

"No problem at all," Mom said. "Allie's in charge of laundry, so you'll have to work that out with her."

"Mom pays me two bucks a week."

"How about I double that?"

"Deal."

While I cleared the table, Mom served apple pie. We never had dessert during the week, but it was an unusual night. My parents were in the same room and actually being nice to each other.

"I'm in charge of cleanup," Dad said. "Maybe Allie could help me."

Mom was happy to put her feet up with a good book.

Dad washed the dishes while I dried and put them away. "Tell me about Sam," he said.

I hugged the plate I was drying to my chest. The same feeling washed over me as when I had first started wearing a bra. I was embarrassed.

Dad scrubbed the pot and waited.

Sometimes when I didn't know how to put my feelings into words, I wrote them down. That's what gave me the idea to show Dad my interview with Sam. "Wait here. I've got something I want you to read."

When I got back, Dad had finished the dishes. He wiped his hands on a towel, sat down at the table, and reached into his shirt pocket for his reading glasses.

I took a seat across from him and chewed my thumbnail.

Dad chuckled as he read my article. "Sam and her dad arm wrestled for the last burger, huh?"

I nodded.

He read the last sentence out loud: "'Whether on or off the court, Sam Johnson makes every day more interesting at Daniel Boone Middle School.' Do you still feel that way?"

"Yes."

Dad laid the newspaper down. He reached across the table and patted my hand. "I understand," he said.

"You do?"

"Yes, growing up with your uncle Jeffrey taught me a lot."

My embarrassment turned into the biggest feeling of relief in the whole universe. Somebody finally understood, and even more important, that somebody was my dad. My eyes filled with tears, and I didn't even care. Dad's eyes filled too and melted part of the iceberg. "Mom doesn't understand about Sam."

"We should probably see a family counselor," Dad said. "Will you do that for me?"

"Will the counselor try to change the way I feel?"

Dad shook his head. "I'll screen counselors ahead of time and make sure we get a good one."

"But you refused to see a counselor when Eric died."

"I know. Cut me some slack, Allie. Adults make mistakes too."

"Not this time, Dad. This time you got it just right."

Dr. Nichols

A few days later, Mom and Dad picked me up from school early. The counselor's office was in Winston-Salem in a two-story brick building. We perched on chairs in the waiting room, nervous, like birds ready to take flight. Dad had already explained that Dr. Nichols wanted to talk to me alone.

"Allison Drake," the receptionist called.

Dr. Nichols's office had a desk, but she didn't sit behind it. Instead she sat in a chair facing me. She was about Mom's age with black hair pulled back into a bun.

"Allie, I've spoken with your dad on the phone, but I'd like to hear directly from you. Why are you here?"

"I think . . . no, I know, well, at least I'm pretty sure, I'm gay."

Dr. Nichols focused her dark brown eyes on me. "How does that make you feel?"

I rolled that question around in my mind like pizza dough. "Happy when it's just Sam and me, but sad the rest of the time, especially around my mom."

"Tell me more about your mom."

I spent the next twenty minutes talking about Mom, about Eric's death, Dad leaving, the day I met Sam, and everything leading up to right then. "I was scared the night Sam ran away. Worried Sam was hurt and that I'd hurt Mom."

"And since that night?"

"I've been lonely. I miss Sam."

"How do Sam's parents feel about all of this?"

"They don't know, at least not for sure." And then I explained about One True Way.

"I always advise patients that safety comes first. Sam needs a place to live and to finish her education. If she feels coming out would jeopardize those things, then perhaps she should wait." Dr. Nichols rested her chin on her fist. "Exploring sexuality is a confusing time for most adolescents, but I am not overly concerned about you, Allie. You are doing just fine."

"Really? I mean, that's a huge relief, but if I'm doing fine, why is Mom so upset?"

"Because parents have hopes and dreams for their children, and sometimes those hopes and dreams don't match the ones kids have for themselves. Do you understand what I'm saying?"

"That Mom is disappointed."

"Yes, but what about you, Allie? Aren't you disappointed in her too?"

I shook my head no, but tears leaked from my eyes. Deep down I knew the answer was yes.

Dr. Nichols looked down at her notes. "We made good progress today, Allie. What I'd like to do next is have you sit in the waiting room while I talk to your parents. Would that be okay?"

I nodded. "They need to talk about Eric too."

"I'll keep that in mind," she said.

My parents were mostly quiet on the car ride back home. Mom's eyes were red so I knew she'd been crying in Dr. Nichols's office.

Dad weaved through expressway traffic with ease. After riding with Mom for so long, it was nice. "Can you turn on the radio?" As I stared out the window, Simon & Garfunkel's "My Little Town" played. The song had a melancholy sound to match my mood. It reminded me nothing had changed in our town. It was about twenty years behind New Jersey.

"Do you think we should consult another therapist?" Mom asked.

"I like this one," Dad said. "What do you think, Allie?"

"I like her too."

As Dad drove west away from the city, there wasn't nearly as much traffic. It seemed like a good time to talk. "What did Dr. Nichols have to say about me?"

"She was mainly trying to get to know us," Dad said. "She did more listening than talking."

"It was the same with me."

Mom caught my eye in the rearview mirror. "Dr. Nichols said with enough love and communication, we can be closer than ever."

That's what I wanted too, but right then it seemed as impossible as being with Sam.

By the time we got home, I was tired of being analyzed and ready to be a normal kid again. "Can I walk to Phoebe's house?"

Dad raised his eyebrows at Mom. "Is that okay with you?"

Mom tucked a strand of hair behind her ear. It was graying at the roots. I'd never noticed that before. "That's fine, but be home in time for dinner," she said.

I ran toward Phoebe's, filling my lungs with gulps of fresh fall air. I didn't think she'd mind that I was showing up uninvited. Her grammy always had plenty of cookies. I climbed the steps to the front porch, knocked, and waited.

When Sam opened the door, I had a surprise even better than fresh-baked cookies. A big smile spread across her face to match the one on mine. We couldn't help it; just being in the same place made us happy.

"Come on in," Sam said. "Phoebe is pouring the milk and Grammy's taking cookies out of the oven."

"What kind?"

"Macadamia nut."

We took our milk and cookies to Phoebe's room. She cleared away yarn and crocheted caps so we'd have a place to sit. "I'm still trying to convince Sam to ride in the Pioneer Days horse show," she said.

"Has Penny's leg healed enough?" I asked.

Sam nodded.

"Then you should do it."

"Will you be there to watch me?"

"Yes." Ribbit, ribbit.

"Ribbit, ribbit," Sam answered.

"You're both weird," Phoebe said.

"And you're our friend," Sam said. "That makes you weird too."

Phoebe laughed. "I guess it does. You're going with Webb, right?"

The smile slid from my face. "Yeah."

"You don't seem too happy about it," Phoebe said.

"I'm not, but I don't want to hurt his feelings."

"He's a great dancer," Phoebe said. "I danced with him a couple times last year."

From the way Phoebe looked when she talked about Webb, I knew she would've loved going with him. It was too bad he'd asked me instead of her. I munched on one last cookie. "I have to go. I promised Mom I'd be home in time for dinner."

"I'll walk you part of the way," Sam said.

My mood ring turned violet.

Walking in the Rain

It started to drizzle, but Sam and I took our time. It reminded me of a song, "Laughter in the Rain." I started to hum.

"I was thinking about that song too," Sam said.

A lot had changed since the last time we had talked. I wanted Sam to know everything. "My dad got a new job and he's moving here."

"Are you happy about it?"

"Yes."

"Then I'm happy too."

"That's not all. My parents took me to see a counselor today."

Sam stopped walking. Her eyes widened like a frightened deer.

"No, it wasn't like when you talked to the youth leader at One True Way. It was good."

Sam shook the raindrops from her hair. "Nothing could be as bad as that."

"The counselor is supposed to help us learn to be a family again—a family that doesn't live together. That's what my parents said."

"At least your parents know. I can't talk to mine."

"Dr. Nichols says safety first. That you shouldn't tell if it would get you kicked out of the house, or only make your life harder."

"They wouldn't kick me out, but the counselor they'd take me to see would be someone who'd try to reprogram me into a different kid. That's what scares me." Sam stopped walking. "Allie, don't look so serious. Watch this!"

She splashed through a puddle, just like a little kid. I laughed and followed her.

Sam turned and grabbed both my hands. "I wish you weren't going to Pioneer Days with Webb."

Webb. The mention of him always ruined

everything. "I know, but Pioneer Days will still be fun. I can't wait to watch you ride Penny."

"Yeah, that will be the best part." Sam dropped my hands and stuffed hers in her pockets. "I gotta tell you something too."

It was bad news. I could tell by the way Sam frowned. "What is it?"

"Coach and Miss Holt are moving away after the holidays."

"But why?"

"I don't know exactly, but I bet it's because of Mom and One True Way. Coach said it's complicated. I always hate it when adults say that."

"Me too. It's what my parents said when they told me they were separating. Why can't adults just tell us the real reasons?"

"They forget how to listen too," Sam said. "My parents don't understand me at all."

It started to rain harder. We kept talking until we were both drenched. "I better go before we drown in the storm or Mom sends out a search party."

"You're right," Sam said. "Bring Penny some carrots to the horse show."

"I will. 'Bye, Sam." Ribbit, ribbit.

"Ribbit, ribbit," she answered.

During the rest of my walk home, I thought about Sam, and then Coach and Miss Holt. Why were they moving away? I needed to know the real reason.

I went early to our next newspaper staff meeting so I could talk to Miss Holt alone. It was tricky because we'd never discussed her relationship with Coach Murphy before.

I sat at a desk facing her and chewed on my pencil.

"Stop that. You'll ruin your teeth."

"You sound just like my mom."

Miss Holt smiled. "Since I like your mother very much, I'll take that as a compliment."

"Are you really moving away?" I blurted out.

Miss Holt blinked a couple times. "I wasn't expecting that question, but yes, yes we are."

"But why? All the kids love you, and Sam really counts on Coach."

Miss Holt blinked again, but this time she was blinking back tears. "We, Murph and I, don't have the support of some of the parents, and it would be difficult for the administration to stand behind us."

"Is it because . . ." I wasn't sure how to put it into words without embarrassing her or crossing some forbidden line.

"We really shouldn't discuss this any further," Miss Holt said. "If Murph and I leave without making a fuss, we've been promised good recommendations. That's the best we can hope for."

"We've got to do something!" I said. "I'll ask all the kids to write letters to the principal and the school board. I'll—"

Miss Holt shook her head. "No, Allie. The more attention you draw to Murph and me, the less likely it is we'll get the good recommendations we've been promised. And without those, getting other teaching jobs will be difficult."

Dr. Nichols had said safety first, but I hadn't realized it applied to adults too. "But where are you going?"

"To a city. Living under small-town scrutiny doesn't work well for people like us."

If it didn't work for two adults, two twelve-year-olds

didn't stand a chance. I needed to talk to Dr. Nichols. Somehow Sam and I had to change before bad things happened to us too.

A week later, it was back to Dr. Nichols's office. I sat facing her in the same brown leather armchair I'd sat in last time. I had thought a lot about Coach Murphy and Miss Holt. How they had to either move or lose their jobs without recommendations. "Is being gay a choice?"

Dr. Nichols answered my question with a question. "Did you choose how you feel about Sam?"

"No, it snuck up on me, but if I tried really hard, maybe I could make myself like boys." I'd started wearing a rubber band around my arm, and every time I imagined kissing Sam, I snapped myself with it.

"I've treated patients who conformed to what society expected of them."

"Do you think I should do that?"

"That's ultimately up to you. How much happiness are you willing to give up to fit in?"

That was an even bigger question than the one I'd asked. "I'm not sure. I just want to be happy again, and I want everyone else to be happy too."

"You are not responsible for making everyone else happy," Dr. Nichols said. "What I've observed is that repressing your feelings is like putting a lid on them. If you do, you'll never know exactly how much love you are capable of giving or receiving."

I liked what Dr. Nichols said, but in my case she was wrong. Since Eric died and Dad left, I *was* responsible for making Mom happy. And to be honest, it wasn't just about Mom. I didn't want to suffer like Coach and Miss Holt. Being gay was too hard.

Pioneer Days

Pioneer Days started on Friday night. Main Street was barricaded, so cars had to park on the side streets. The merchants lit their shops with kerosene lamps and dressed in old-fashioned clothes. Most of them served apple cider or coffee. I was saving my costume for the next day.

Webb reached for my hand. "Hungry?" he asked.

"Yes." My heart didn't beat faster like when I was with Sam, but it was still nice.

Webb stopped at one of the booths and ordered hamburgers and lemonades. We sat at a picnic table with Big D and a stuffed collie dog.

"Where did that come from?" I asked.

"Won it at the basketball toss," Dwayne answered. "Thought I'd give it to Jenny. She's in the hospital again."

"That's a stupendous idea," Webb said.

Hearing about Jenny caused sad feelings to gush from my heart and fill my whole chest. I had started donating part of my allowance to St. Jude, and after reading my newspaper article so had lots of other kids.

Big D shot an imaginary basket. "Stripped the net three times in a row. That ball swished through the air smooth as silk. Sam won a dog too. Gave it to her little brother."

One mention of Sam and my heart beat faster. I looked down the crowded street, but there was no sign of her. "Where's the horse show?"

"The big field beside the community center," Webb said. "It'll start tomorrow morning." He pulled the program out of his jacket pocket and took a look. "At ten o'clock."

Webb and I finished our burgers and shuffled down Main Street. I kept my eyes peeled, hoping for a glimpse of Sam. Little kids bobbed for apples, and we stopped to watch for a while. The air was full of good smells: cotton candy, caramel apples, salty pretzels, and funnel cakes.

We strolled toward a bluegrass band playing on a stage at the end of Main Street. "Why are you wearing a rubber band around your wrist?" Webb asked.

Trying to think of a good excuse, I snapped myself with it a couple of times. "Uh, um, I was helping Mom organize her files and forgot to take it off."

The fiddle moaned a sad song about a girl who died young. A few couples danced in front of the stage. Webb reached for my hand again. "Want to dance?"

I watched the other couples over his shoulder. Melissa was dancing with a dark-haired boy. She had her eyes closed and a dreamy smile on her face. I should have felt that way about Webb, but I didn't.

When the song ended, Melissa caught me staring at her. Our eyes locked. She knew I'd rather be dancing with Sam. Melissa grabbed her boyfriend's hand and headed toward us. She probably hated me for being with Webb. I didn't blame her.

Mom got there first. Her face was glowing. "Allie, Webb, I loved watching you dance! Practicing together really paid off."

Melissa listened and watched.

My brain couldn't make my mouth work. I wanted to scream at Mom, to beg her to stop. But I froze. I wanted to tell Melissa that I still liked Sam, but kids like us turned into adults like Coach and Miss Holt, adults that got hurt. But I didn't. I didn't say a word.

Mom reached into her pocket and pressed ten dollars into my hand. "Here, I want you to have a good time this weekend."

Melissa shook her head. When she turned away, I almost went after her to explain. Almost.

Webb walked me home around nine o'clock. We climbed the steps to the front porch, and I reached into my pocket for the house key.

"I had a great time tonight," Webb said.

"Me too." It seemed like the polite thing to say, but it hadn't been a great night—more like okay.

Webb pushed his glasses up on his nose. "Saturday is the best part of Pioneer Days. Nearly everyone will be in costume. The horse show is a bit smelly, but the square dancing is stupendous."

Why did he have to be so fussy? The horse show

would smell like a barn: hay, manure, and leather. It would remind me of learning to ride Penny. "I have an old-fashioned dress for tomorrow. I borrowed it from Sam's sister."

"I bet you'll look beautiful in it." Webb bent down and kissed my cheek. "See you tomorrow, Allie."

No racing heart, no sweaty palms, no tingling cheek. Nothing. Was it possible for me to change? Did I even really want to? I put my arms around Webb's neck to find out.

His eyes nearly bugged through his glasses, and his shoulders shook. I screwed up my courage and kissed him.

"Allie," he breathed, "that was mag . . . magnificent."

His sweet smile, and the way he stuttered "mag . . . magnificent," made me feel like the biggest traitor since Benedict Arnold. "Oh . . . oh no!" I rushed into the house so he wouldn't see me cry.

Allie Drake–
Horrible Person

The community center was about a half mile away from downtown. I could have walked, but Mom insisted on driving me. "I wanted to talk to you alone," she said. "Without Dad."

I popped my wrist with the rubber band a couple of times. "What about?"

"Dad will be moving into his apartment next week."

I wanted to curl into a little ball and cry. Instead I shrugged.

"Allie, it's okay to be sad."

I couldn't talk to Mom about all the pain punching holes in my heart. Dad moving out again made me anxious, like when Sam was lost. And the way things turned out for Coach and Miss Holt made me afraid of growing up gay, but kissing Webb had been the opposite of magnificent. It had been a lie.

"Dad will still be close by," Mom continued. "You can walk there every day if you want to."

I didn't want to see Dad. I didn't want to see anybody. Not Webb or Sam either. I was too confused.

Traffic crawled toward the community center. We finally came to a dead stop behind a long line of cars. "This is close enough. I can walk the rest of the way."

Mom reached out and patted my arm. "I hope today is as much fun for you as last night. I loved watching you dance."

Mom had seen what she wanted to see. That made me boiling mad! Why didn't she look deeper?

"Dad's moving is hard for me too," Mom said. "I had hoped we could work things out."

"Then why didn't you try harder?" I snapped. "When Eric died, it was all about the two of you.

And now it's not about *me*, but the way you feel about Sam and me. Why don't my feelings ever count as much as yours?"

Mom looked as stunned as if I'd slapped her. "I'm sorry, Allie. Children don't come with an instruction manual. I'm doing the best I can here. It's one of the reasons we're seeing Dr. Nichols." Mom slammed the steering wheel with her fist. "Maybe we should skip Pioneer Days and go home."

"No! I don't want to go home with you. I have a date with Webb."

"Allie!"

I slammed the car door, and instead of going to the horse show, I ran toward church. Reverend Walker knew about Mom and Dad. She was Coach and Miss Holt's friend, and she'd been there the night Sam ran away. If anybody could help me, she could.

Our church had gotten into the spirit of Pioneer Days. A red wagon was parked out front, holding bales of hay, pumpkins, gourds, and dried corn. I kicked the wagon wheel. Hard. A sign on the front said, COME YE THANKFUL PEOPLE COME. I was not thankful.

I hurried around back to Reverend Walker's office. She stood staring out the window, as if she'd been waiting for me. "Come in, Allie. I like your dress."

I took a couple deep breaths to calm down. "Melissa let me borrow it."

"I was just headed over to the horse show," she said. "I'm surprised you're not already there."

"Could we have Russian tea?"

"Of course we can." Reverend Walker busied herself, filling the kettle with water and putting it on the hot plate.

I waited until we both had our mugs. "Maybe I should start at the beginning. I went to Pioneer Days with Webb last night."

"And . . ."

"We had hamburgers and listened to a blue-grass band."

Reverend Walker sipped her tea.

"My dad's moving into an apartment. That makes the things I'm going through even worse."

"I know. Your mom has been worried about telling you."

"Everything fell apart when Eric died."

"Grief never completely goes away," Reverend Walker said, "but it lessens over time. At least that's been my experience."

"Did Mom tell you we're seeing a family counselor?"

"Yes, I recommended Dr. Nichols because your dad isn't comfortable with pastoral counseling."

"I hate that Coach and Miss Holt are leaving. It worries me."

"Me too. More than you know."

"What happened to them made me want to change. I even asked Dr. Nichols about it."

Reverend Walker's hands tightened around her mug. "What did she say?"

"That repressing my feelings would be like putting a lid on them. That I'd never know how much love I was capable of giving or receiving."

Reverend Walker smiled her angel smile. "What a lovely way of expressing it. I wish I'd said that."

"I kissed Webb last night."

Reverend Walker's eyebrows arched, but that was the only sign she was surprised. "Is that why you're here?"

"No, I'm here because I exploded at Mom, but I

guess the reason I exploded was because of all of them: Eric, Mom, Dad, Coach, and Miss Holt. I had too many bad feelings inside."

"Why did you kiss Webb?"

"To see if it would make any difference. Kind of like an experiment to see if I could be like most other girls."

"Then what happened?"

"Webb said the kiss was magnificent, but I felt ashamed, like I'd played a dirty trick on him. Does that make me a horrible person?"

"No, just a confused one."

"I'm tired of being confused."

"I bet if you look deep inside, you already know the answer."

"Yeah, but what if there's no good answer? I'll hurt people I care about either way."

"Pray about it, Allie. That's the best advice I can offer."

I prayed. I knew prayers didn't come with a guarantee, but they couldn't hurt.

The Horse Show

When I got to the horse show, Sam was riding in the Western Pleasure class. I'd never watched her in a real horse show before. She was dressed in chaps and a cowboy hat. I could have stared at her all day.

The horses walked, jogged, and loped. The judges were looking for a horse that seemed pleasurable to ride. That's how the class got its name.

Webb walked up beside me and looked down at his shoes. "I was afraid you weren't coming."

"You mean because of . . ."

"Yes, I, uh, don't have a lot of experience, so maybe I didn't do it exactly right."

I scuffed my shoe in the dirt. Poor Webb had

probably worried all night. "I'm the one who kissed you, remember? Maybe I didn't do it right."

Webb pushed his glasses up on his nose. "I thought it was magnificent."

I shouldn't have kissed him, but I wasn't sure how to take it back. "I was late because I stopped by Reverend Walker's office. It took longer than I thought it would."

"Whew!" Webb blew out a big gust of air. "I'm glad to hear that."

I didn't want to hurt his feelings, but I didn't want to be alone with him either, not even in a crowd. I scanned the bleachers for some of our classmates and saw red hair glistening in the sun. It was Phoebe! "Come on, Webb."

We climbed the bleachers, and Phoebe scooted over to make room for us. She didn't take her eyes off the horses, but patted her jacket pocket. "I brought some carrots for Penny," she said.

Sam had asked me to do that, but I'd been so worried about kissing Webb that I'd forgotten. I was grateful Phoebe had turned out to be my friend. Not only for the carrots, but for making a date with Webb seem more like a normal day.

The announcer called the riders to the center of the ring. The three judges walked in front and in back of the horses, taking notes. One of them asked for Penny to back up. She took four steps backward, just like she was supposed to.

"I bet Sam's gonna win," Phoebe whispered.

I chewed on my thumbnail. If Sam won, maybe it would make up for basketball, at least a little bit.

The announcer awarded the white ribbon for fourth place.

Then the yellow one.

And the red one.

Sam had either won first place or nothing at all.

The announcer said, "And the blue ribbon goes to Miss Sam Johnson, riding Penelope's Pleasure."

Phoebe and I squealed and threw our arms around each other! I hadn't been this proud of another person since . . . since Eric's last baseball game.

"Don't I get a hug?" Webb joked.

Phoebe was the one who hugged him.

After Sam collected her ribbon and posed for pictures, we headed for the horse trailers.

"Hey," I called. "Congratulations!"

"Thanks," Sam said, but she didn't smile or look happy to see me. My reporter's antenna went up.

Phoebe stopped beside Penny and pulled a carrot out of her pocket. She wrapped her hand around it, the same way Sam had shown me. I had thought it was something special, something just between us. My grateful feelings toward Phoebe didn't stop me from being jealous. Not one bit.

"Great job out there," Webb said. "When is your next ride?"

"Egg and Spoon is in a couple of hours," Sam said.

"That gives us time to stop by the community center," Webb said. "See if Phoebe's grammy won a ribbon for her cookies, and more important, if she brought extra cookies for the official Friends of Phoebe Club."

Phoebe laughed. "She did bring extra cookies, and we can stop by the crochet display. I won a ribbon earlier this morning."

"Y'all have fun," Sam said. "I need to stay with Penny."

It wasn't like Sam to miss spending time with us, and her dad was close by. "Why can't your dad watch Penny?"

Sam crossed her arms over her chest. "I'm the one who rides her. It's my responsibility."

"Oh." Ribbit, ribbit.

Sam didn't croak back. Why? She always answered me.

Phoebe led the way toward the community center. I turned and looked back at Sam. She was hugging Penny.

What was wrong? I needed to talk to Sam alone.

Saying Good-bye

Long tables lined the community center. Each one had a sign in front of it. They said things like HOMEMADE JELLIES & JAMS, CANNED PICKLES, QUILTS, and EMBROIDERY. I barely paid attention. All I could think about was the way Sam had buried her face against Penny. I remembered what she'd told me: *Horses don't judge. Penny doesn't care that I dress like a boy, or about my report card, or if I miss the winning basket. Penny just loves me.*

We munched on cookies from Phoebe's grammy that had bananas and chocolate chips in them. Webb and Phoebe were on their second cookies already.

"I adore cookies," Webb said. "These are stupendous!"

"Nobody likes cookies more than Webb," Phoebe said. "When we were seven or eight, he dressed up as the Cookie Monster for Halloween."

"And you were the Little Red-Haired Girl from Charlie Brown," Webb added.

The whole conversation seemed stupid. Something was wrong with Sam. That was all that mattered.

A couple of women around my mom's age stood admiring Phoebe's crocheted afghan. "Phoebe," one of them called. "I was just telling my friend about you."

"Mrs. Owens's shop might sell some of my work," Phoebe said. "I should stay and talk to her. How about we meet back at the bleachers in time for Egg and Spoon?"

We agreed, and that left me where I least wanted to be—alone with Webb.

The two of us kept weaving our way among the displays. Wood carving was my favorite. An older gentleman with a long gray beard sat beside the table. Wood curls fell from his whittling knife. "What are you making there?" Webb asked.

"When I get 'er done, it'll be a robin."

While Webb chatted with the whittler, I pulled the ten dollars Mom had given me from my pocket. I bought a small carved horse and waited while a lady slipped it into a bag.

"Webb, I'll be back in a few minutes. I want to give this to Sam for good luck." He was so fascinated by the man's wood carving that he only nodded in my direction.

I hurried away from him and toward the horse trailers. Sam sat on a bale of hay, picking at a ham-and-cheese sandwich. "Stale bread?"

She shook her head. "I'm not hungry."

"What's wrong?"

"Nothing."

"That's not true. Talk to me, Sam."

"Okay, but not here."

We walked the length of the field and stopped by the woods. I opened the brown bag I was carrying and handed her the horse. "I bought this for you in the community center. It's for good luck."

Sam ran her fingers over the horse's mane. "Did you kiss Webb last night?"

I had only fainted once in my life—after Eric's funeral—but I had the same sick feeling. "How do you know that?"

"Webb told me. He was worried when you were late this morning, and since we're friends, he thought I might know how you felt about kissing him."

"It was an experiment."

"This is not science class, Allie. Webb likes you, and so do I."

"I wanted to test whether being gay is a choice. Feeling this way is hard. Look at what happened to Coach and Miss Holt. My mom's unhappy, and you're too scared to even tell your parents."

"Did you *like* kissing Webb?"

"No. It felt like a lie!"

Sam shook her head. "Then why are you here with him?"

"Because I promised, and he's my friend." Sam didn't understand. I wasn't sure I understood myself, except there was no easy way out.

"You have to tell Webb the truth, Allie." Sam handed me back the horse. "I don't want it. I'm sorry I made things hard for you."

I closed my fist around the horse and squeezed. "I just want to be happy without hurting Mom, and without ever going through the kind of stuff that's happening to Coach and Miss Holt."

"But you probably would," Sam said, "or something similar." Her dark eyes flooded with tears. "I can't change who I am, but maybe you can."

My eyes filled with tears too. "I'm sorry. I wish I was brave enough to be your girlfriend, but I'm not."

Sam's hands trembled, and she balled them into fists. "I'm still glad you liked me back. At least for a little while."

I remembered that day in the barn when the sky had been bluer than blue. "I'm glad too," I whispered.

Sam turned and walked away from me, without once looking back.

"Wait!" I yelled. "Wait!"

But Sam was too far away to hear me.

Egg and Spoon

After Sam walked away, I stared down at the carved horse. Just looking at it made me cry. I used my shoulder and hurled it like a baseball pitcher, far, far into the woods. I tried telling myself this was for the best, that if Sam's parents knew, it would be a disaster. Even so, I was miserable. A lonely ache squeezed my heart.

I stared into the woods for a long time. Finally, I went back to the fair. I washed my face in the community center bathroom. I practiced fake smiling in the mirror. Like when Eric died, nobody could see the pain inside. I checked my wristwatch. It was almost time for Sam to compete in the Egg and Spoon class.

Webb and Phoebe were waiting for me in front of the bleachers.

"What took you so long?" Webb asked. "I was afraid you'd miss the show."

"Just looking around. I love all the costumes!"

"They are pretty great."

"Have you ever watched an Egg and Spoon competition?" Phoebe asked.

"Not a real one, but I did help Sam practice."

"I've been helping her practice too. She's even better than last year."

Sam probably did like Phoebe more than me, and if she didn't, she probably would soon.

The horses and riders entered the ring. I tried not to look at Sam, but I couldn't help it. She was handsome in her Western clothes.

The class started out slow. The horses walked while each of the ten riders balanced an egg in a spoon. On the second time around the ring, the first rider dropped her egg. "It's harder than it looks," Phoebe said. "Sam let me try."

Sam had never offered me that chance. Never.

The announcer called for a trot. Sam and the

other riders bobbed in their saddles. It didn't take long before two more riders dropped their eggs.

"Lope your horses," the announcer called. The horses picked up speed. They made it around the ring once, and then three more riders dropped their eggs. Plop, plop, plop.

"Only four riders left," Webb said. "I bet Sam will take home another blue ribbon."

I hoped so. Sam deserved something good to happen.

"Reverse," the announcer called. The riders turned their horses and rode counterclockwise around the ring. I couldn't stop staring at Sam. She glanced in my direction, and that's when her egg fell.

The disappointment on Sam's face made a noose around my heart and squeezed.

"Her concentration was off," Webb said. "Sam was looking in the stands instead of paying attention."

It was all my fault.

"She'll still get a white ribbon for fourth place," Phoebe said.

But Sam hadn't been practicing all those weeks

for fourth place. I didn't care what happened after that, but we stayed until the class was over. We watched Sam accept the white ribbon, and then the yellow, red, and blue ribbons were handed out.

"I'm starved," Webb said. "How about we walk over to Main Street, grab a ham biscuit, and listen to the Battle of the Bands?"

"You two go ahead," Phoebe said. "I'm gonna stay and talk to Sam."

I followed Webb because I was the last person in the world Sam wanted to see. I had ruined everything.

The square dancing started at eight o'clock. All of the display tables had been cleared away, and the community center doors were thrown open wide.

"The music here is always stupendous," Webb said.

A tall, mustached man played the banjo, and a pretty woman with long flowing hair played the fiddle.

"I'm a fan of all genres, from classical to country. If it has a beat, I'll dance to it," Webb said. He held out his hand. "Ready?"

"Not yet. Could we get something to drink first?"

"Stupendous idea," Webb said. "I'll get us some apple cider."

That gave me time to look around. Mom was having a deep conversation with Reverend Walker. I could tell by the serious look on her face. Melissa was with her boyfriend again, and Sam's mom was helping at the refreshments table.

While I sipped my cider, Webb tapped his foot to the music. Mr. Johnson called, *"Pick up your partner, and whirl her around."* I remembered the afternoon I had danced with Sam. We had been so nervous, but it had been perfect.

The next song was played to the tune of "Skip to My Lou." I let Webb lead me onto the dance floor. We whirled and twirled, around and around. When the music stopped, I got my first look at Sam. She was dancing with Jonathan, but she wasn't smiling.

Between songs, Phoebe asked me if she could dance with Webb. "I really like to dance, but since I don't have a date, I could be waiting all night for somebody to ask me."

"Sure, go ahead." She'd actually be doing me a

favor, but I kept that part to myself. "Hey, is Sam really upset about finishing fourth?"

"Not about fourth. She's mad about not doing her best."

I shouldn't have been staring at Sam, but I couldn't help it.

While Phoebe and Webb danced, Mom trudged over.

"I'm sorry about this morning."

I shrugged.

"You don't look happy tonight."

She had finally looked deeper. I was miserable, but it was hard to find the right words to tell her exactly how miserable. I remembered my conversation with Dwayne. *Sam is about my favorite person around here.*

Mine too.

Then tell your mom that.

Why did speaking up have to be so hard?

Mom touched my arm. "To be completely honest, you haven't looked happy in a while."

I had a lump in my throat the size of New Jersey. "Yeah." Ribbit, ribbit. "I saw you talking to Reverend Walker."

"She told me you stopped by this morning. She would never betray your trust, though."

I looked past Mom at Sam and Jonathan.

Mom turned to see what had my attention.

"You still like her, don't you?"

If I answered yes, it would hurt Mom, but if I said no, it would be a lie. Reverend Walker had said God didn't want me to live a lie. "Being with Sam makes me happy."

Mom's eyes got teary. "It's okay with me, Allie. Truly. It will just take some getting used to." She wiped her eyes with her fingers. "Sam's leaving. You'd better go."

"I can't. I'm here with Webb."

"I'll tell him you had to leave. He and Phoebe make a cute couple."

"Really?"

Mom nodded. "Really. What I want most of all is for you to be happy, Allie. I love you."

"I love you too!" And that was the truth. No matter how many times we all messed up, we were still a family: Dad, Mom, Eric, and me. Not even death or divorce could change that.

I pushed and shoved my way through the crowd. "Sam, Sam," I called.

She couldn't hear me over the music and the noise.

Dwayne tried to talk to me, but I didn't stop moving. "Not now, Big D."

Reverend Walker waved me over, but I only waved back and kept pushing.

When I finally got to where Sam had been, she was gone. My heart fell flat, like a cherry coke with no fizz, but only for a second. I would find Sam if it took all night. I had to!

Just Sam

I ran outside, but Sam had disappeared. There were a few people leaning against cars in the parking lot, but not Sam. My heart raced. Jonathan! Or Melissa! Maybe one of them knew where Sam had gone.

I hurried back inside. Melissa was square dancing, so I knelt down to talk with Jonathan. "Sam went to check on Penny, but she'll be right back."

Penny! I should have thought of that. Sam and Penny had a barrel racing competition the next morning.

Lifting my long skirt, I rushed back outside. The lantern lights kept me from tripping, or stepping in horse manure.

When I got close enough to see her, Sam was

hugging Penny. She spoke to her in such a low voice that I couldn't make out the words.

I waited until Sam finished talking. "It's me."

Sam gasped and her eyes widened. "What are you doing here?" Her voice cracked.

"I had to tell you I'm sorry."

"You already said that."

"And . . . and I wanted to ask you if we could back up. If we could go back to that day in your barn when I gave you the friendship bracelet and you said you didn't like anybody else as much as me."

"A lot has happened since then."

I thought about how scared I had been the night she ran away. How my heart had broken when Mom didn't understand, the hopeless feelings when Sam had quit the basketball team. I thought about Coach Murphy and Miss Holt, and how I was still scared about the future. But mostly I remembered my last session with Dr. Nichols. "My counselor said I could pretend my feelings for you don't exist, but then I'd never be as happy as I could have been. I don't want to be like that."

"Me either, but it's complicated."

I always hated when adults said that, but it

turned out to be true. Liking Sam was messy and complicated.

"Aren't you worried about hurting your mom?"

"Mom is coming around." Sam's parents probably never would, but I didn't say that out loud.

"Are you sure about this?" Sam asked. "What about Coach and Miss Holt? Being gay is hard."

"I know." I took a deep breath. The answer was deep inside, just like Reverend Walker had said it would be. "But not being myself is even harder. Mom and Dad will help me. I know they will."

Sam smiled in the lantern light. "Then maybe we need to start over."

"You mean back to the very beginning?"

"Yeah." She stuck her hand out like a politician. "Just call me Sam," she said. "I know all the kids at DB, so you must be new."

I shook her hand. "Allison Drake." My voice came out all scratchy like I had a frog in my throat.

"Ribbit, ribbit," Sam said.

"Ribbit, ribbit," I answered. I was usually shy around people I didn't know, but something about Sam felt different, right from the start.

Author's Note

We are all living through history, but we may not realize the significance until years later. I was a teenager
in the 1970s and remember watching Anita Bryant's
commercials for the Florida Citrus Commission. She
sang, "Come to the Florida Sunshine Tree." You can
still watch these commercials on YouTube.

It wasn't until writing this book that I realized
Anita Bryant had also played a role in denying equal
rights to homosexuals. She became a spokesperson
against a local ordinance in Dade County, Florida,
that prohibited discrimination based on sexual ori-
entation. Bryant's Save Our Children campaign led
to a repeal of the ordinance, and in 1977, Florida

legislators passed a bill that prohibited gay adoption. That law remained on the books until 2015.

Bryant went on to lead campaigns around the country that denied equal rights to homosexuals, but her actions negatively impacted her career. Many people boycotted products for which she was a spokesperson.

On her website, Anita Bryant Ministries International, it states, "I made a stand not against homosexuals as persons, but against legislation that would tend to 'normalize' and abet their lifestyle, and would especially afford them influence over our children who attended private religious school."

Due to the actions of Anita Bryant and other like-minded people, the 1970s were a time when gay and lesbian teachers could lose their jobs and when kids who liked each other the way Sam and Allie did kept it a secret or were shunned.

I have a special connection to this story. When I was in my early twenties, my best friend told me she was gay. I had never been more stunned in my life. My reaction was much like Sam's sister, Melissa's. I struggled to understand how someone I was so close to had kept that big a secret. I wondered if I knew her at all. But I came to understand the courage it took to tell the truth, and that my reaction was the problem. My friend was the same person she had always been. I was the one who needed to change.

I wrote *One True Way* to make sense of that period in my life. My hope is it helps young readers navigate a difficult topic, whether they are gay themselves or have friends who are.

It would be impossible for a book to mirror the experiences of every gay person, but I hope I've done this topic justice. Prior to publication, a minister, a lesbian, a gay man, and the mother of a gay son reviewed *One True Way*. All of these people helped shape Sam and Allie's story.

The following books were invaluable to me: *Defrocked: How a Father's Act of Love Shook the United Methodist Church* by Franklyn Schaefer, *Crooked Letter i: Coming Out in the South* by Connie Griffin, and *When Christians Get It Wrong* by Adam Hamilton.

Speakforthem.org states that "suicide is the leading cause of death among Gay and Lesbian youth nationally." These teens need to see themselves in books. They need to know they're not alone.

Acknowledgments

It truly takes a village to turn a story idea into a published book. The 2014 National Council of Teachers of English (NCTE) Convention provided the spark that became *One True Way*. I got up early to hear my editor, Andrea Pinkney, speak on a panel. During the session, the moderator talked about the lack of middle grade books dealing with homosexuality. I knew immediately that I wanted to write such a novel. I owe a round of applause to NCTE!

Lots of people offered input. I'd especially like to acknowledge Rob Sanders for suggesting the Anita Bryant connection; Nancy Stewart for her prompt feedback; Kendra Gayle Lee for sharing painful episodes from her growing-up years; Lorin Oberweger, who pointed out that Allie would make a more compelling character if she had a goal; and the Reverend Vicki Walker, who talked theology with me and pulled a copy of *Defrocked: How a Father's Act of Love Shook the United Methodist Church* from her personal bookshelf.

One True Way couldn't have found a better home than Scholastic. A giant hug to Andrea and her whole team! And as always, I'm grateful for the contract expertise of my agent, Deborah Warren.

And finally, my deepest gratitude to all the students, teachers, and librarians who have read my novels. I get the chance to live my dream because of you.

About the Author

Shannon Hitchcock is the author of the critically acclaimed *Ruby Lee & Me*, a nominee for the 2017–2018 Nebraska Chapter Book Golden Sower Award, and the Crystal Kite Award-winning *The Ballad of Jesse Pearl*, both hailed for their immediacy and cadenced voice. Shannon's picture book biography, *Overgrown Jack*, was nominated for the Sue Alexander Most Promising New Work Award. Her writing has been published in *Cricket*, *Highlights for Children*, and *Children's Writer* magazines. She divides her time between Tampa, Florida, and Hendersonville, North Carolina.